I0524819

SNOT-NOSED ALIENS

STORIES FROM PULPHOUSE FICTION MAGAZINE

Edited by
DEAN WESLEY SMITH

Snot-Nosed Aliens

Published by WMG Publishing Inc.
Cover and interior design copyright © 2019 WMG Publishing Inc.
Cover art copyright © by ralwel / Depositphotos

ISBN 13: 978-1-56146-092-2
ISBN 10: 1-56146-092-3

CONTENTS

INTRODUCTION

TOO MANY ALIENS

When you ask a bunch of professional writers to send in stories to a *Pulphouse Fiction Magazine* anthology called "Snot-Nosed Aliens," you get a bunch of really, really strange stories, which is exactly what I had been hoping to get.

And I already had four stories that I loved and wanted in this book. And the publisher of WMG Publishing had given me a strict word limit of how large this book could be.

So in come the stories. Forty-six strange and wonderful stories to be exact. Depending on length, I could buy eight or so more stories out of those forty-six. Yikes!

And all the writers were professional, so all the stories were good.

Double Yikes!

Luckily, I also had regular issues of *Pulphouse Fiction Magazine* I could buy stories for as well, and that helped ease the pressure some. But still, I had a lot of aliens. Way, way too many great alien stories, fun alien stories, weird alien stories.

In other words, I was a very lucky editor and I knew it. The writers had made my job difficult by sending me far too many great stories. But after a bunch of time shuffling and swearing and laughing, I managed to get this crazy project down to thirteen alien stories.

They are all original to this volume and a final reward for everyone who supported the *Pulphouse Fiction Magazine* Kickstarter campaign that helped us get the magazine going almost two years ago. So thank you for your support.

Pulphouse Fiction Magazine is going strong and I am having a wonderful time finding great stories for both the magazine and for fun books like this one.

I sure hope you enjoy these original stories. I sure did.

—Dean Wesley Smith

THE PROBLEMATIC NAVIGATION OF THE VESSEL CLAYTON BOOKER

J. STEVEN YORK

J. Steven York's stories always make you think and have heart. This one, about an alien hiding on a human space ship is classic J. Steven York.

Steve not only has had a story in every issue of Pulphouse Fiction Magazine *so far, he is also doing a really fun and off-the-wall internet comic for every issue on the back page. Don't miss either Steve's wonderful stories or his comic.*

Through the senses of the vessel, I closely observe the actions of the attendant that had just entered the chamber. The attendants were useful. They provided sustenance to the vessel. They cleaned it. They provided it nourishment. They assisted with the removal of its wastes. They were vital to the progress of my mission on this planet.

But their constant close proximity and interest in the vessel also meant a constant threat of exposure and the probable destruction of myself. Likely the vessel as well, though that was only of practical importance. I could certainly move to another vessel, I had done so before. But I had to do so without discovery, and I could not allow myself to be discovered or somehow captured. To my knowledge, I am the only one of my kind to have reached this world. I must assume that full weight of the mission lies with me, until the time—very soon I assure myself —that I can create duplicates of myself and introduce them to other vessels. Soon, with numbers, we will be unstoppable. But for the moment, I remain vulnerable.

I struggle to identify the individuals of this planet's dominant life form, and that this is even necessary is a facet of my difficulty. These beings are not uniform or interchangeable. The services provided by the attendants was not uniform either. Some were attentive, careful, and prone to social interactions I still struggled to understand. Others were sloppy and distracted in ways that could be harmful to the vessel. Some were actively hostile, often in unpredictable ways. Some had even harmed the vessel, lashing out for unknowable reasons of their own, or in response to some evident misstep by the vessel.

The behaviors of these beings were deeply motivated by elaborate and contradictory social constructs that were nearly impossible for me to understand. In time, they would be eliminated, but until then, navigating them was my greatest challenge, and my greatest danger.

I recognize this particular attendant from its small stature, and the distinctive crown of reddish orange hair on top of its head. Also the talons on its manipulating appendages, its hands, which were artificially colored red. This was one of the attentive ones, the social ones. An advantage, but also a potential problem. I turned the vessel's eyes to meet the attendant's own, something I had learned was an important social gesture, though it was meaningless to me.

The attendant glanced down, and tugged at the fastenings of one of the fabric coverings that these beings wore to compensate for their lack of natural thermal protection. "Mr. Clayton," she sounded, "did you button this shirt yourself?" The corners of her food and sound hole moved upwards in a way that might be significant. "You got the buttons wrong again, dear." She began to unhook the fastenings and refasten them in a different order. The corners of her food hole contorted even farther. "But at least you fastened them yourself today. That's good. Progress!"

I noted the sounds, only some of which I was able to assign any meaning to. While my vocabulary was growing rapidly, the language was complex and arbitrary. The meaning of those sounds, even when I thought I clearly understood, could change according to circumstance and other cues I did not understand. The contortions of the face, the movements of the food hole and the eyes, seemed especially important, as did the tone, pitch, and volume of the sounds, but I had no clear grasp of why or how.

Satisfied with my coverings, she leaned back and looked at the vessel. "Lunch is in an hour. We're having ham today. Do you like ham?" I did not have the vessel react other than to look at her. I could make the vessel speak, and it was sometimes useful, but my efforts more often led to confusion and negative social reactions. Silence and passivity were generally safer. "I'm sure you like ham. I'll come back for you then. Do you need to go potty?"

I recognized the nature of the interrogative, and "potty" as one of an unnecessarily large lexicon of sounds associated with the voiding of waste from the vessel. I did not sense the need, and so attempted the most basic communication I knew, moving the vessel's head from side to side. This seemed to satisfy the attendant. "Maybe after you eat," she sounded. She moved toward the door. "I'll be back, sweetie." It slipped out of my chamber and closed the door behind it.

When she was gone, I pushed the vessel out of the movable platform on which it rested and brought it to a standing position. I flexed the upper limbs, and lifted first one foot, then the other. My ability to balance and move the vessel grew daily, as did the vessel's strength and dexterity. The molecular changes I was carefully making to the vessel's metabolism were slowly reversing its decrepit state. When I had first occupied it, I judged it to be near the end of its natural lifespan, even ignoring the diseased state of its brain. Now I was reversing this, at least enough for my purposes.

In physical terms, the vessel was becoming quite capable, something I did not yet wish the attendants to know about. I was not yet ready to move to the next phase of the mission. There was too much to learn about the social puzzle of these creatures and their communication, and the pods that I would use to replicate myself in other vessels were not yet ripe. But I had drifted through space since before these beings had evolved from less complex forms. I am patient. I have all the time in this world.

———

The vessel stopped on the far edge of the feeding chamber, standing near the transparent wall that covered one side of it. It shifted its weight, almost of its own volition, to rest on the assistance device, a *cane*, that the attendants had provided to help with walking. In truth, I retained it more out of appearance than necessity. I did not want the attendants knowing how strong the vessel had become, how capable. Though it was obvious that the vessel's condition had improved, I had to keep up the illusion of fragility.

Through the vessel's eyes, I looked out of the structure, at a world I had only experienced in diminished form, through the senses of a procession of previous vessels, lesser creatures that burrowed or crawled or slithered or flew. Through them I had learned the fundamentals of how life operated on this planet, and how to maintain and improve it. Perhaps it had been an error to have skipped some of the larger and more intelligent life-forms, but I had seized an opportunity. The habitual opening of another transparent wall in the vessel's sleeping chamber, through which my flying vessel was able to enter. There, I had found this vessel and its fortuitously diseased brain which I was able to enter, study, and slowly consume.

The attendants had eventually found the old vessel, of course, the small, flying creature behind the sleeping platform, its stiff, desiccated body hidden behind the vessel's sleeping platform, its broken skull and empty cranium a source of some interest. But that quickly passed and seemed forgotten, the old vessel disposed of in the metal cylinder where non-bodily wastes were always placed.

Through the transparent wall I could see a roadway, during daylight often busy with mechanical conveyances and this planet's natives moving about individually, at night, less so. I studied everything I could see: the structures, the patterns of movement, the sounds, the millions of social interactions that seemed to shape everything. I had no doubt that I could navigate the vessel out of this structure and into that flow of traffic, but it was still a mystery what I would do when we got there. Where would I find shelter or sustenance for the vessel? Where else could I find such suitable vessels as in this place, hosts with diseased brains and salvageable bodies?

Outside the structure a flat, rectangular obelisk stood covered with a symbolic, visual form of these beings' language. I studied and imagined the sounds. "State Veteran's Home." I struggled with the sounds. "State?" Condition? "Home?" A place of dwelling. That was clear enough. But "veteran's?" The possessive form I understood, but "veteran?"

Riffling through the fragmented memories and pathways I have salvaged from the vessel's brain, I find an association with a fighter. A soldier. But I have seen no soldiers here. Only attendants of various sorts, and the residents, broken and diseased beings at the end of their span. They are not fighters. In fact, I remain puzzled why the residents are even kept alive. Could they not be consumed as food, or at least terminated so as to not be a burden on stronger beings?

Puzzled, I withdraw my attention into the vessel, and to the portions of diseased brain I have not yet consumed. There are yet useful memories and pathways here to be decoded, and I have limited my own growth to allow for its orderly consumption. As I eat what is left, I record each portion's chemical and quantum states, and then catalog these for later organization and processing.

The disease that destroyed the vessel's original function fragmented those memories and the pathways that allowed the brain to think, remember, and process. Painstakingly, I have been sorting what is left, piecing together broken links and fragmented memories, finding potentially useful parts, and incorporating them into my own matrix. It is through this that I have learned what I have of the vessel's language and social structure, and hope to learn more.

To do this, I must fight my own hunger and the instinct to grow. I must preserve what remains of the vessel's brain and process it in an orderly fashion. I filter nourishment and oxygen from the vessel's fluids, but nothing is more satisfying than feeding directly. And ultimately, I must have the space and energy needed to develop the pods through which I will disperse. This skull is vast compared to the last one I occupied, but there is never enough room.

But I must move on. I must prepare this world for the creators. I do not know when they will come, but I know they will, even as I know they sent me so long ago. I must replicate myself into more vessels. I must act undiscovered until I have the numbers to move openly. Then all these beings must become vessels to serve the creators. It is imperative. It is my reason for existence. It must be done.

I sort through my matrix, finding the locations most associated with "veteran," and begin to consume them, following the paths as I do. I am rewarded with nourishment, a bit more space for myself and my pods, and a flood of related fragments of thought. I was never expected to incorporate so much of the vessel into myself, but given the complex organization of the *"humans/people/dudes"*—the related sounds appear in my matrix, an accidental byproduct of my search—I have no choice.

More pieces come together. "Veteran." An individual who is experienced. A *former* soldier.

Understanding. Could this vessel have once been a young,

strong, and capable fighter of its species? Ironic, as it has now become a fighter for my creators.

"I see you standing here all the time, looking out? What are you looking for?"

I turn the vessel in the direction of the sound. To one side, I see a small—human—sitting in a motorized conveyance. One of its lower limbs is missing, and I judge it also to be late in its lifespan, though perhaps not so much as my own vessel. Like the attendant of the orange head covering, it is small and lumpy about the upper torso in a way that seems important. Its head covering is silver grey, and like the attendant's has some length and volume.

But though it is a bit younger, I cannot salvage its incomplete body, and it seems to have a high-functioning brain that will resist an attempt to occupy it. It is useless to me as a potential host, and therefore of no interest. I turn back to the transparent wall.

"You don't have to talk," sounded the person next to him. "My husband used to say I talk enough for two people anyway." She made a noise that I knew conveyed an emotional state I did not understand. "I know you almost never talk. But I see you, and I wonder if you're lonesome inside and want somebody to talk to you."

I do not respond, hoping the being will lose interest and leave.

Idiot.

The sound, and the meaning, seem to come from nowhere. Doubtless, it is a product of the brain I have just been consuming and processing. Idiot. Diminished in intelligence or capacity. But the urgency of the realization puzzles me. The being talking to me does not seem to be an idiot. It seems one of the more intelligent and articulate residents I have encountered in this place.

Idiot.

She.

Woman.

More understanding. These—people—have two reproductive genders. This is somehow socially relevant. This annoying example is a "she," a "woman." Not previously knowing this makes me—an idiot? No. Merely innocent of the fact, ignorant, uninformed, unaware. Something that is now corrected.

The *woman* though, continues to make sounds at the vessel, faster than I can really understand or process. I am inclined to continue ignoring her. I consider moving the vessel completely away, to the waste disposal room, or to its resting chamber.

But I sense I have learned something important, this distinction between the sexual forms of these people. Perhaps, in this case, it is worth risking some kind of engagement. I turn toward—*her*—and make eye contact. I struggle to find the sounds, to articulate the complex plumbing of the vessel's food hole in order to make them. "I—" The vessel croaks, not sounding quite right. I try again. "I—Clayton Booker." Clayton Booker is the individual designation of the vessel. I have learned that the exchange of such designations is a frequent opening of social interaction.

The woman's food hole—(*Idiot. Mouth!*)—contorts in response. "My name is Liana," she sounds. "Liana Jackson. Glad to meet you Clayton."

I do not know how to respond. With some effort, I contort the corners of the vessel's food hole upward.

———

The woman is patient and eager to teach. I have learned more about language and social interaction from her in a few tens of day cycles as I have in the many hundreds that have preceded it. I have consumed much of the vessel's remaining brain tissue, as her interactions have allowed me to more rapidly and effectively process and assimilate it.

But she is also an impediment to my activities. She is most always there when I leave the sleeping chamber. She takes nourishment when the vessel does. She takes note of my movements, and seems concerned when I direct the host to do anything unusual or outside its expected parameters. And yet, my need to exceed those parameters grows. If I am to leave this place and continue my mission, I need to make preparations. The host will need—*clothing*, and *shoes* for protection from the outside elements, and to blend into the people. I will need portable stores of nourishment and water to sustain the host while I look for independent sources outside this—home.

And I have recently learned from the woman of another complication of this society of people. They have some manner of abstract transactional system used to obtain useful items and services. I need something called *money*, a kind of physical token that is key to this system. I have learned that most people carry money, but they guard it closely as a matter of survival, and it will not be easy to obtain.

I may need to resort to violence, and I do not desire the attention that that will inevitably draw. The woman may have money. I will attempt to request that she give it to me, or perhaps I can terminate her in some way that will not draw attention. Several times since I have been in this vessel, other residents of this place have ceased living, and while it causes brief alarm, it does not seem to be unexpected and seems quickly forgotten. This process may be useful. I will attempt to learn more.

I draw upon my store of information, and consume more of the remaining brain tissue. As I consume, there is more room to grow and increase the capacity of my thought matrix. Though I must also allow for the growing replication pods, I am still able to record and reintegrate memories and pathways with increasing speed. The process gives me satisfaction, or perhaps it is just the effects of increased nourishment and yet another burst of growth.

But then I find something I do not expect.

Run.

I feel a sudden tension, a feeling of danger and alarm.

Run.

Something about the residents who are terminated, their bodies taken away, something I cannot quite grasp.

I watch as people walk past the open door of the vessel's rest chamber. I pay special attention to the attendants. The one with the orange hair and red claws that I now know to be a woman. The large, volatile, sometimes violent one that I now know to be a male like my vessel. Two other males that seem to be of higher rank than the others. A larger female with dark hair who seems to occasionally cause pain to residents when other attendants are not present.

Run.

I feel there is a threat there. Not a *new* threat, but one that has always been there, and that I have failed to recognize. I have previously wondered why the useless and broken creatures in this place were not terminated or consumed. Now I see that they are. Just not all at once. This is not a place to care for the useless. It is to *store* them until they are needed or perhaps until they simply are in the way.

Then they are culled.

I see it now. How did I not see it before?

Run.

I move the vessel as quickly as I can to gather the supplies I have collected. Shoes and a small bag of clothing taken from an attendant storage area. Packaged sustenance bars hoarded from past feedings and taken from the rooms of other residents.

I need two more things, and they will be the most difficult

to obtain. I leave the sleeping chamber and wander the corridors. I must find the woman Liana Jackson.

I begin to wonder if she has already been culled when someone grabs the vessel's arm from behind. I spin the vessel to see and it stumbles, nearly falling. The vessel's arm extends automatically to brace against the wall. It is surprising how much the vessel's nervous system can still manage on its own. I turn the vessel to see. It is the Liana Jackson. Her face contorts in a way I take to be a positive emotion, but it is complex, and I am not sure.

"Clayton! I was looking for you! I wanted you to know, you won't see me for a while. My granddaughter is having a baby! And they've invited me to stay for a month or so—to 'help out' they say. I don't know how much help I'll be at my age, and with my leg and other problems. But I so want to see that baby! It's my first!" She touched the vessel's arm. "I wish you could tell me if you have grandchildren, or even children. I hope so, Clayton." She turned away and then back. "I have to go. My son-in-law is picking me up any time now."

I struggle through the sounds. So much of it is meaningless, social connections that are meaningless to me. But I understand that the Liana Jackson is leaving, and I must accomplish my goal quickly. "Money," I sound, as she starts to turn away.

She turns back. She makes a mouth sound. "Oh, honey, I have money! I get my checks, and mostly my daughter and their son will pay for everything."

She does not understand. I struggle to articulate the proper sounds. I have the vessel gesture toward its own torso. "*Me,* money. Me!"

She tilts her head. "Oh, honey, you don't need money. They won't even let you use the vending machines. You don't think you're going with me, do you? No! You have to stay here! I'll be back before you know it."

"Money!"

Her food hole contorts another way. She reaches into a fold of her garment. "Look, I don't know why you think you need money, but here's a dollar. It's all I have." She pressed a fibrous rectangle covered with pictures and symbols into the vessel's manipulator—*hand*. Then she half turned, already walking away, "I'll bring pictures! Maybe even videos!"

Then she is gone.

I should have terminated her to obtain more money, but we were in a hallway, and too many attendants were nearby. I look at the rectangle. I do not know the trade value of a "dollar." Perhaps it will be enough. I stuff it into the storage fold of one of the vessel's garments.

I return to the rest chamber and collect the bag that contains what I have gathered. Now I need only to leave the structure, and I have discovered that all the doors to the outside are kept locked. Only an attendant can open them, and I have observed that they appear to open them using a hard rectangle that most of them wear on a loop around their upper bodies. I must obtain such a rectangle.

I start to leave, but the vessel's hand reaches for the walking assistance stick, the cane, that leans by the door. I pull the hand back. I do not need the stick, and it will only impede the vessel's movement now. Then I reach again. I have directed the vessel unconsciously. I do not understand the compulsion.

I extend the hand again, pick up the cane, and examine it. Why do I need it?

Weapon.

The lower part of the cane is made of a hard plant material, but the upper part on which the hand rests is made of metal. I have the vessel grasp the cane in both hands. I twist, and the upper parts turns, loosens. I continue to turn it, and the upper part falls away. It is heavy, hard, and fits the vessel's hand well. It is small enough to be easily hidden. It has a right-angle bend in the middle, and the part that extends from the hand forms something like a short club. It is small enough to conceal, and I will be able to hit something quite hard with it without damaging the vessel's hands.

Weapon!

I slide the piece into a storage fold of a garment and move away from the common areas of the home. In the back of the structure are places for the attendants, where nourishment is prepared, garments are somehow refreshed, waste containers are taken, and other work is done. There will be doors to the outside there. There will be attendants with opening cards.

The last meal of the day is done, so I choose the food preparation area. I open the door slowly. There are lights and noise, but I can see nothing but the metal benches and shelves where the nourishment is processed. There are smells, and the vessel responds to them, desiring substance, primitive instincts stirring in the torso, preparing for the processing of nutrients. I ignore them.

Moving on, I hear noise of moving water, the clanking of hard objects, and someone making mouth sounds, a single voice sounding in that ritually rhythmic way that humans seem to find interesting and diverting. There are words, but I do not understand any of them.

A lone human, an attendant I have never seen before, works at a basin full of water and some kind of white foam. It—he— washes residue from the round platters on which food is brought to the residents. He does not see the vessel, or hear its approach.

I take out the hand end of the cane. I raise the vessel's arm high. I bring it down with all the force I can on the skull of the attendant. There is a short cry of alarm, and the human begins to slump.

I strike again.

Again.

Again and again.

The skull is harder than I imagined. I realize it will be difficult for me to break out of this one when the time comes, when the pods must be introduced into new vessels.

I look at the vessel's hand and the weapon held there, smeared with red bodily fluids. I had not anticipated that. I dunk the hand and the weapon into the water, sloshing it around, turning the foam pink. Some of the fluids have washed off, but not all. It will have to do

I cause the vessel to kneel and pull the card from the attendant. He does not move, but I can see respiration. I do not have time to terminate him.

I move farther back, finding a door. There is a raised panel next to it, and I hold the card over it as I have seen the attendants do.

"Hey!" The sound comes from behind me. "What you doing!" Someone is moving toward me.

Then I hear them stop.

"Shit! Juan! What the fuck he do to you, man? Juan, you hear me?"

The new threat seems distracted. I rush through the door. I am on a concrete platform outside. There is a railing, and steps. To my surprise, water is coming from the sky. The vessel shivers. The organs that had just been anticipating nourishment, now rumble and convulse in distress.

The closing of the door is slowed by some mechanism. Through the opening I hear the voice sounds. "You run, you fuck! I'm calling the fucking..."

The door clicks shut, the sounds cut off.

Run!

I move the vessel as quickly as I can. I am in a narrow passage between two structures. There are few windows, and the doors are all closed. But beyond, I can hear the sounds of vehicles moving through the precipitation and standing water. I walk toward the sound, hoping there will be other humans, and I can hide myself among their numbers.

I emerge between the building to a path full of vehicle traffic, but there are no people. I move away from the State Veteran's Home as quickly as I can. The vessel protests. I feel its primal urge for shelter, explaining why there are no other people on the street. I am exposed, but I must keep the vessel moving for now.

A large vehicle moves quickly past, and splashes through collected water, which showers onto the vessel. Autonomic alarms sound. The vessel fights my control.

Idiot. Coat.

The word sounds come from nowhere. From inside me. For the first time, I feel fear. I question my own actions, my own decisions. So many things I could have done better. The mission!

More sounds. Loud, wailing sounds. I have heard them before, but I do not know what they mean. They come closer.

Idiot.

The sounds grow louder, closer. So much sensory input. So much confusion. I struggle to understand. I seek more of the brain to consume.

It is gone.

Idiot.

I know now. I have consumed too much. Assimilated too much of it into my matrix. I feel the rain. The cold. The pain. Images flash. Faces. Word sounds. Touches. Louder voices. A far-away place. Heat. Fear. Danger. People sound in alarm, in pain. Limbs explode into red mist. Heads explode. Humans terminate. And then time passes without danger. Without pain. Only memories. Until, finally, the memories slip away...

And I have found them.

A vehicle veers from the flow and stops on the path in front of me. Lights flash on the top. Doors open. Humans climb out, in matching dark garments, shining bits of metal glinting as they move. Another kind of attendant?

"Sir, put your hands where we can see them!"

I don't understand. The vessel's hands are in the folds of its garment. I did not move them there. I feel the handle of the cane, and close the hand over it.

The people in the dark garments point their arms at me, metal objects held tightly in their hands. They are too far away to strike me with them.

"Sir! Get down on the ground, hands behind your head. *You know the drill! Get down!*"

Another vehicle stops, blocking the path behind me. More loud mouth sounds. A sense of alarm that comes both from the vessel and from within.

"Raise your hands! Get down on the ground! Get down on the ground!"

Another vehicle next to me. I am boxed in. I do not know who to do.

Weapon.

I will the vessel to remove its hands from the folds of the garment. I still hold the handle of the cane. I will need to get closer to use it. I step toward the nearest human.

"Gun! Gun!"

"He's got a gun!

"Gun!"

Loud noises. The vessel's torso is yanked three directions at once. Another blow, to the arm, causing the upper part to rip open, fluids squirting out, the top of the cane falling from the fingers.

More loud noises, on and on, until there is clicking. Finally, even that stops.

The vessel tumbles forward, and then sensation fades. My body shakes as some final blow hits, perhaps the vessel's skull striking the ground. But not hard enough to break. *Not hard enough to break!*

There is no sensation but my own. The vessel is gone. Dead. I realize that respiration has stopped. The fluids do not flow. *There is no oxygen!*

I struggle, within the skull, my prison, I convulse with all my might. But it is useless.

The bone is too hard. It will take hours to dissolve. I am doomed.

The pods.

The mission.

I am alone, in my final moments. Alone in the dark.

There is only the voice. Taunting.

Goodbye.

Idiot.

BLUE-EYED BOMBSHELL

ANNIE REED

Annie Reed is a regular in Pulphouse Fiction Magazine *and you can understand why with this original take on comic and science fiction conventions.*

Annie's stories appear regularly in many varied professional markets and I am proud to say she is also a regular contributor to Fiction River.

Her story "The Color of Guilt" was selected for The Year's Best Crime and Mystery Stories 2016. *She is also one of the founding members of the innovative* Uncollected Anthology.

———

The most beautiful woman Sandy had ever seen in her life was decked out in blue fur from the neck down.

"I think I'm in love," she muttered.

The woman in question couldn't hear her, of course, thanks to the press of people crowded into the lobby of the San Jose Convention Center.

Early-bird registration for DigiCon was in full swing, and Sandy was stuck working the booth for the general admission lines. The blue-furred bombshell was in the VIP line on the other side of the lobby with about a billion people in between them.

And yes, bombshell was definitely the right word for her. With her long, luxurious blonde hair and shapely (not skinny) figure, she looked like she'd stepped right off one of those retro posters that decorated the walls of Sandy's favorite restaurant in San Pedro Square.

Except, you know, for the fur.

DigiCon was one of the largest anime conventions in California. Dealers, artists, and voice actors—along with a few minor television stars—and about ten thousand fans all crammed together for three days of photo ops, autographs, cosplay contests, and shopping, shopping, shopping.

Sandy had volunteered at DigiCon for eight years, and this was the biggest one yet. She'd already checked in someone who came all the way from Montana. Amazing that people would come from that far away just to go to a con.

In all that time, she'd never seen such a gorgeous woman, blue fur or no blue fur.

With any luck, Sandy might actually get to meet her sometime during the weekend.

When she wasn't working.

The next group in Sandy's line were a family of five. Mom and Dad looked shell-shocked already, and the con hadn't even really started yet. The three kids—two tweenage girls wearing Pokemon T-shirts and one little brother dressed like a Ninja Turtle—looked like they couldn't wait to ditch their parents.

Sandy'd never considered bringing her own mom to one of the cons. Her mom's idea of a good time was curling up on the sofa with a good book. The most she ever said about Sandy's interest in anime cons was that she hoped Sandy would find a nice girl at the con one day and settle down. Sandy would settle for a girlfriend who didn't make her feel like a dork for loving anime cons.

The teenagers who made up most of Sandy's registration line came in mostly groups of twos and threes and one time a group of six, all tall, skinny boys who wore variations of *Dragon Ball* Z costumes, right down to spiky-haired wigs, and more body spray than should be legal.

Two of the guys gave Sandy smiles that were no doubt meant to be sexy come-ons. Sandy was used to it. Even though she was twenty-eight, she still looked like she was a senior in high school, and a short senior at that.

She wanted to tell the boys to ditch the stinky body spray if they wanted to stand any kind of a chance in hell of getting a date.

Not with her, but they didn't know that.

When she finally got a break in her line, she bent over to rub her sore feet. She'd be working in the dealer hall tomorrow. Six hours of standing on a concrete floor on Cosplay Day. Her feet might never forgive her.

At least she wouldn't be wearing heels.

Con volunteers were "encouraged" to dress in some sort of cosplay outfit the first full day of the con. She hadn't done that the first year she'd volunteered, and she'd been razzed unmercifully. She'd dressed up every Cosplay Day after that.

This year she'd opted for comfort over sex appeal. Of course. The one year she might want to attract a little attention from a certain blue-furred attendee, Sandy had decided to cosplay as a S.T.A.R.S. officer from the Resident Evil video games. Black pants, black combat boots, dark gray shoulder pads, gray beret, and absolutely no skin showing.

"I have a question," a smooth, silky, sexy-as-sin voice asked.

Sandy straightened up—almost bashing her head on the booth in the process—and found herself looking right at the blue-furred woman. She was standing right in front of Sandy's booth, one hip cocked at a provocative angle.

Sandy swallowed hard.

Not only was this woman absolutely gorgeous up close—deep blue eyes, dramatic cheekbones, full lips—she was the most unusual furry Sandy had ever seen. A fair number of furries attended the con every year. Most either covered themselves entirely in baggy fur topped off with an oversized animal head, or they settled for a full-head furry mask and fur-covered gloves.

This woman, though. Beneath a gauzy, semi-transparent gown of shimmering aquamarine, she was entirely covered in form-fitting blue fur from her neck down. No fur on her face, only blue-painted eyebrows. Her smooth skin had a pearly sheen that made her look a little pale, but hell, Sandy's own complexion ran to the "never seen daylight" side of the spectrum.

And near the top of her head, she had two fuzzy blue ears.

She was stunning. Tall, yes—about a foot taller than Sandy —but absolutely stunning.

So stunning, in fact, that Sandy nearly forgot how to use her words.

"Uhm...a question?" she managed to finally blurt out.

The vision in blue fur grinned. "One of those things people sometimes say that isn't a statement."

Sandy felt her cheeks heat up. Way to make a great first impression.

"Right," she said, smiling around her embarrassment. "What can I help you with?"

"I didn't get a program in my bag." The woman opened her VIP swag bag. Sandy couldn't help but stare at her long, delicate, fur-covered fingers. "Do you happen to have any to spare?"

Sandy had a whole stack of program booklets. She handed one over.

"Thank you," the woman said.

Think, Sandy told herself. She should say something— anything—so this woman wouldn't think she was a total space case.

Only her mind was a complete blank. She couldn't come up with *anything* except...

"Have a great con!"

How totally lame was that! Sandy wanted to take the words back as soon as they left her mouth.

But the woman's face lit up with what looked like genuine pleasure. "Thank you." She held out her hand. "Bianca."

Sandy introduced herself as she took the woman's hand. "Nice to officially meet you."

The fur on the woman's glove felt wonderful. Soft and silky, not stiff like most costume fake fur. Sandy could almost feel the slender bones in Bianca's fingers.

"Your costume's awesome," Sandy said. "Is it from anything I'd recognize?"

One of the fuzzy ears on top of Bianca's head cocked forward just the tiniest bit.

Wow. Good animatronics. Sandy'd seen animatronic ears for sale in the dealer hall at past cons, but she'd never seen anyone use them to such great effect.

Bianca gave her an enigmatic grin. "It's a character of my own creation. Glad you like it."

She took her hand back, and Sandy realized that she'd been holding it far longer than a simple handshake required. Oops.

"I imagine I'll see you around the con," Bianca said.

"I'll be here all weekend."

Bianca raised one eyebrow and leaned across the booth toward Sandy. "Do you get time off for good behavior?" she asked, her voice a low, sexy purr.

Well, alrighty then. This could be fun.

"I get time off even for bad behavior," Sandy said with a wicked grin of her own.

Bianca rewarded her with a gorgeous smile. "Good to know."

They were both leaning toward each other now, Bianca bent low enough she was almost the same height as Sandy. Any closer and they probably could have kissed.

Before Sandy decided to do just that, someone behind Bianca cleared their throat.

Bianca glanced over her shoulder, and for the first time Sandy noticed a guy dressed just like Bianca, right down to the fuzzy blue ears in his longish blond hair. He was tall like Bianca and wore billowy pants that weren't quite as transparent as her gown. His pants were pulled in at the ankles, which made him look like a furry version of the genie from *Aladdin*. Every other visible part of him except his face was covered in blue fur just a shade darker than Bianca's.

"Did you design that costume, too?" Sandy asked.

"In a manner of speaking," Bianca said.

The blue-furred guy looked impatient.

"I'd better go," Bianca said, straightening up. "Don't worry," she said with a wink. "We'll run into each other again."

Sandy watched them until they got lost in the crowd. They'd looked very comfortable with each other, and he'd definitely looked possessive. Dammit.

She didn't have long to regret not stealing a kiss when she had the opportunity. A sweaty guy in a *Tokyo Ghoul* T-shirt shuffled over to her table. "I... uh..."

He pushed his thick, black-rimmed glasses up his nose. He seemed stuck, his expression caught between confusion and exasperation, and he wouldn't quite look her in the eye. His T-shirt looked brand new, his pale complexion was flushed, and he was carrying far too much in his overstuffed backpack. That backpack was going to knot his back up like crazy by the time the con was over on Sunday.

Had to be his first rodeo. He'd learn.

Sandy put on her best Helpful Con Volunteer smile and turned toward the sweaty new guy. He didn't smile back.

"What can I help you with?" she asked.

———

Sandy didn't see Bianca again until late the following afternoon.

Dressed in her S.T.A.R.S. officer cosplay outfit, Sandy had spent her day staffing the con's information booth, conveniently located smack-dab in the middle of the dealer hall and surrounded by more con attendees than she could count.

The dealer hall took up the entire arena in the convention

center. The huge, cavernous, concrete room was packed to the brim with rows upon rows of vendor booths up front and artist booths near the back. The information booth was the size of a small mall kiosk, and the only booth accessible on all sides to the attendees.

The information booth gave Sandy a great view of the surrounding aisles. When the aisles weren't crammed full of people taller than she was.

Her job consisted mostly of handing out lip balm and hand sanitizer branded with the con's logo, helping attendees figure out where to go for panels and meet-ups, and generally keeping an eye out for any potential problems.

Not that that was easy to do when more than half of the attendees were cosplaying, and more than half of the cosplay costumes included weapons of one type or another. At least the weapons all sported a bright yellow zip-tie provided by staffers at the Peace Bonding booth whose job was to assure that any cosplay weapons *were* fakes.

Sandy had hoped to see Bianca early that morning during the half hour VIPs were allowed in the dealer room before the general admission hoard streamed through the doors. Bianca did have a VIP badge, after all.

But no go. Even though the dealer room had been relatively empty during that half hour, Sandy hadn't caught site of any furries at all, much less Bianca or her blue-furred friend.

To say she'd been disappointed was an understatement. She'd had the most unusually vivid dreams about Bianca the night before, dreams that started with discovering what was underneath all that fur.

She'd consoled herself with a bag of kettle corn from a nearby vendor while she people-watched between answering questions and handing out con freebies. The other con volunteer at the information booth, a nice kid named Jason she'd worked with before, kept up a constant stream of chatter, but

Sandy gave up trying to listen after a while. What with the crowd noise bouncing off all that slick concrete, not to mention competing K-Rock songs blaring from various vendor booths throughout the dealer hall, it was just too hard to carry on a decent conversation.

She did see Sweaty New Guy a few times. Once she'd watched him buy a T-shirt, this one for *Assassination Classroom*, from a nearby vendor. He promptly shoved the shirt into his bulging backpack. When he finished, he pushed his thick glasses up the bridge of his nose.

She smiled. He was getting the hang of things. She hoped he wasn't too disappointed that the con didn't have any voice actors from *Tokyo Ghoul* or *Assassination Classroom* on the schedule this year.

Finally, just when the crowd was starting to thin out like it always did the last hour before the dealer hall closed up for the night, she caught sight of Bianca and her friend standing with a few other cosplayers in front of an artist's display half an aisle away.

Bianca still wore the same furry costume, right down to the iridescent gown and moveable ears. But under the unforgiving fluorescent lights in the dealer hall, it was pretty clear her fur wasn't just blue. It was aqua and turquoise and cerulean with highlights of the faintest silver.

Sandy probably would have noticed that yesterday except she'd been too intent on staring at the woman's gorgeous face.

The fur Bianca had used for her costume looked like the real thing. If, you know, real fur happened to be multi-toned blue.

Bianca's friend must have said something funny, because she laughed and smacked him on the arm, and one of her ears twitched.

Not swivel, like a hard piece of plastic on a headband. Twitch. Like a cat's.

Sandy didn't know exactly how animatronic ears functioned, but every pair she'd ever seen for sale in the dealer room had a thin, black plastic arm fixed to the headband the ears were attached to. The arm curved around the side of the wearer's face and made her (or him) look like they were wearing an old-school Bluetooth headset.

Except Bianca wasn't wearing one of those controllers.

Come to think of it, Sandy hadn't noticed a black controller thingy on Bianca's friend's face either, and he was still in costume, too.

She was still watching both of them when his gaze locked on something a couple of booths away from where they stood.

And damn if the guy's ears didn't flatten against his head.

Holy crap!

Animatronic ears *definitely* didn't do that!

Sandy stood up on tiptoes—as much as she could in her cosplay combat boots—and craned her neck to see if she could tell what he was looking at. Sometimes being short was a real pain.

From her perspective, everything looked normal enough. Shoppers were giving a wide berth to a wheelchair-bound cosplayer all decked out like a Dalek from *Doctor Who*. The group of six *Dragon Ball Z* guys she'd met at registration the day before stood clumped together in front of a booth with a bunch of busty figures on display. A tall cosplayer in an Assassin's Creed cape had stopped to take a picture of a cosplayer dressed like Dorothy from *The Wizard of Oz*, only this Dorothy held a Chihuahua in the crook of her arm.

The Chihuahua was visibly trembling.

Okay, so maybe something wasn't right here. But what?

When Sandy glanced toward Bianca, the woman's ears were flat against her head now, too. Her gorgeous eyes were narrowed and her mouth was drawn down in a tight, thin line.

The Assassin's Creed cosplayer moved along. Sweaty New Guy was standing on the other side of him.

Only Sweaty New Guy didn't look so sweaty or new anymore.

He looked dangerous.

His thick, black-framed glasses were gone. His shoulders were squared off, his back straight, and his upper body rotated to the left. He held something in his hands that looked like a little black plastic gun, and he stood with his feet apart just enough to maintain balance and his legs bent slightly at the knees.

Sandy recognized that stance. She'd practiced it in front of the mirror on her closet door until she could drop into it at a moment's notice in case someone wanted to take a picture of her in her S.T.A.R.S. cosplay outfit, complete with the black plastic shotgun she wore in a sling on her back.

Sweaty New Guy was in a shooter's stance, but he wasn't in costume and no one was taking his picture.

And the little black plastic gun in his hands *didn't* have a bright-yellow zip-tie from the Peace Bonding booth.

"Hey!" Sandy yelled.

Sweaty New Guy didn't flinch, but nearby attendees looked at her and froze. Sandy realized she was holding her S.T.A.R.S. shotgun at the ready. She didn't even remember reaching for it.

Talk about practicing your shooter stance. She lowered her weapon and yelled at Jason to call Security even as she bounded out of the information booth.

Sweaty New Guy had raised his weapon, which had morphed into something that looked like the bastard child of a laser pulse rifle and a pointy-ended bayonet—toy guns *definitely* didn't do that!—and was aiming toward the booth where Bianca and her friend stood.

Sandy spared a glance toward Bianca. What she saw nearly stopped her dead in her tracks.

Both of them were crouched now on top of an empty table in the artists' alley. Bianca's ears were still flat against her skull, nearly hidden now by her blonde hair, and a tail—an honest-to-God, blue-furred *tail!*—swished back and forth around her thighs.

That was no damn costume.

Bianca and her friend were furries.

Real furries.

At DigiCon.

And Sweaty New Guy was about to shoot them in a room full of hundreds of innocent people.

Well, the hell with that.

Sandy reversed her hold on her cosplay shotgun so that she was holding it by the barrel. It might not be a real gun, but the butt end did have a bit of heft to it.

Bianca and her friend looked like they were about to pounce on the guy with the gun.

Over the screaming and shouting from fleeing attendees, and even over a con staffer's nervous voice on the loudspeaker imploring everyone to remain calm and evacuate aisles D and E in an orderly fashion, Sandy heard a new sound.

A high, whining buzz coming from directly ahead.

Red lights were blinking on one after the other along the side of Sweaty New Guy's weapon.

Son of a bitch.

"Hey, asshole!" Sandy yelled as she barreled through people toward Sweaty New Guy.

He didn't react, but a teenage boy who stood rooted to the spot between Sandy and Sweaty New Guy stared at her with wide, shocked eyes.

She shouldered the teenager out of the way and kept running, her combat boots clomping on the concrete.

Sweaty New Guy finally started to turn toward her.

She didn't break stride. She didn't stop to think that maybe running at a guy holding some weird pointy-ended weapon he was trying to aim at *her* now wasn't such a hot idea.

She just swung her shotgun.

She didn't aim anywhere in particular. Sweaty New Guy was a pretty big target, and if she swung hard enough, she ought to be able to hit him *somewhere.*

The butt end of her gun caught him on the wrist of his trigger hand. Sandy felt the jolt from the impact in both her arms all the way up to her shoulders.

He howled as both their guns went flying.

When he howled, Sandy got a good look at his teeth. He'd only muttered at her yesterday, looking down at his feet the whole time he'd been at her booth. She'd thought he was just an insecure nerd. What he'd really been doing was covering up the fact that he had a mouthful of grimy, pointy teeth that looked like something out of a horror movie.

She had no time to think about it and no time to slow down. She barreled into him at full speed, one small, determined woman versus one pretty damn solid, definitely not human thing.

They both smacked the concrete floor hard.

He got the worst of it. He landed on his back with her right on top of him. The back of his head bounced off the concrete with a solid smack. His eyes lost focus and his breath came out in a whoosh.

"Damn," Sandy muttered.

The guy's breath smelled like he'd never seen the business end of a toothbrush.

Then again, considering the size of his pointy teeth, they probably didn't make toothbrushes that could sustain that type of abuse.

He blinked, and something that looked like a contact lens slid to the side in one of his eyes. Beneath the lens was a blood-shot, elongated iris and a second set of clear lids that blinked side to side.

Holy shit!

Strong hands—blue-furred hands—pulled Sandy to her feet. She looked up, expecting to see Bianca, but she found herself looking into the deep blue eyes of Bianca's friend.

"That was very brave of you," he said.

Sandy couldn't help herself. She glanced down to see if she could spot his tail, but she couldn't see it.

He obviously guessed what she was looking for because he gave her a truly wicked grin.

"Only in times of stress," he said.

Sandy felt her cheeks heat up. For all she knew, trying to catch a glimpse of his tail might be the equivalent of trying to peek at a guy's package.

"You're not stressed?" she managed to say.

She was still stressed. Her heart was beating a mile a minute. Here she was, surrounded by three aliens in the middle of a con, and she'd gone charging at one of them armed with only a toy gun! Good thing she didn't wear any makeup. She would have sweated it off by now.

Bianca's friend nodded toward Sweaty New Guy. "Not anymore."

Sandy followed his gaze, and her mouth dropped open.

Bianca was holding Sweaty New Guy's gun pointed right at him in a very businesslike pose, her finger on the trigger.

He still lay on the floor, snarling and blinking that one eye like crazy. No doubt trying to get his contact lens back in place.

"Uh..." Sandy put one hand out toward Bianca in what she hoped was the universal sign for stop. "You're not actually going to use that thing on him, are you?"

"Only if he moves." Bianca glanced toward Sandy and her ears swiveled forward. "Nice costume. Is it from something I'd recognize?"

Sandy started to explain when she realized Bianca was teasing her.

Of course. She'd asked about Sandy's costume the same way Sandy had asked about Bianca's the day before.

Sandy made a show of looking behind Bianca, clearly checking for her tail.

"Aren't you missing something?" she asked, one eyebrow raised.

Bianca shared a quick glance with her furry friend.

He shrugged. "She's pretty observant for a human."

"She also has good taste," Bianca said.

"Because she's interested in you?"

"Obviously," Bianca said.

"Okay, enough," Sandy said. "I'm *right here*, you know."

The furries laughed. Sandy would have joined in, but there was the whole "holding a gun on a dangerous alien" thing they had to deal with.

And the fact that they were surrounded by a growing crowd of regular old humans who'd come back to see what all the fuss had been about now that it was over.

How were they going to get out of here without more people discovering that Bianca and her friend weren't your typical cosplayers?

The *Dragon Ball Z* cosplayers were standing in the growing crowd. That gave Sandy an idea.

She smiled at one of the teenagers who'd tried to flirt with her yesterday and pointed at her beret where it had landed on the floor in a nearby booth.

"Want to hand that to me?" she asked him.

He bent down and picked up her hat with a flourish. His buddies laughed, and a couple of people in the crowd applauded.

"You're badass," he said to her as he handed her beret over. "You know that?"

"Thanks." She plopped the beret back on her head. "Now how about my shotgun?"

He dutifully retrieved her shotgun off the floor. She rewarded him with a saucy wink, then turned her attention the rest of the people crowded around their little scene.

"Did you like our impromptu skit?" she asked the crowd.

More people applauded. Out of the corner of her eye, Sandy saw Bianca and her friend exchange wary glances.

Trust me, Sandy wanted to say, but she needed to play this out for the crowd, not for them.

"Remember all those signs about peace-bonding your weapons?" Sandy pointed at the bright yellow zip-tie on her cosplay shotgun.

A couple of people in the crowd said yes. One cosplayer with an impressively large scythe made out of cardboard and duct tape waved his weapon high in the air. The blade on the scythe was too big to be zip-tied, but Sandy caught a glimpse of yellow plastic around the handle.

"Peace bonding, yo!" he shouted, and the crowd rewarded him with laughter.

"Well," she said, smiling now as she really got into the part. "At S.T.A.R.S. we take potential threats to your safety and security seriously. So on behalf of DigiCon, I want to remind you that if you don't want to end up like our hapless victim here, be sure to get your weapon—" Sandy pointed at the gun Bianca was holding. "—peace bonded."

More people laughed, and pretty much everyone applauded.

Sandy bowed, holding onto her beret so it wouldn't fall off.

When she straightened up, she saw a couple of guys from security heading toward them through the crowd.

Time to wrap this up.

"Thank you again!" she said to the crowd. "We hope you enjoy the con." Then she turned to Bianca. "Better make yourselves scarce. Security's coming."

The furries shared a look.

"Seriously. Go." Sandy gestured at Sweaty New Guy. He'd managed to blink back his contact lens so both his eyes looked human again. He'd also lost his dangerous demeanor. Maybe he was only really dangerous when he had a weapon. "I can explain him. I can't explain you two."

Especially not if other people had seen their tails.

Bianca gave Sandy a long look, then she touched the tip of her blue-furred index finger to the point of Sandy's chin.

Time seemed to slow down. The people around them moved at a snail's pace. Crowd noise took on a lower pitch. For a second, Sandy felt like she could see every individual strand of blue hair in the fur beneath Bianca's chin.

Her own chin tingled in a curious and definitely not unpleasant way.

A flicker of gold light flashed in the depths of Bianca's blue eyes. "You don't have to explain any of us," she said.

Sandy blinked.

Time sped back up. The crowd noise regained its normal fervor. The scent of sweaty bodies and kettle corn assaulted Sandy's nostrils, but the tantalizing promise of blue fur and gold-flecked blue eyes was gone.

Bianca, her friend, and Sweaty New Guy had all disappeared.

———

Sandy managed to talk her way out of any serious trouble with con security.

She told the stern-faced head of security—one of the two men who'd founded DigiCon nearly ten years ago, as a matter of fact—that she'd thought she'd seen someone threatening two furries with his weapon. Which wasn't peace bonded.

"That's no reason to tackle someone!" the head of security told her.

It helped that no one was around to lodge a complaint against her. Whoever—or whatever—Sweaty New Guy really was, he'd only cosplayed at being human. He was gone now. Sandy hoped never to see him again.

Bianca, on the other hand—Sandy was really going to miss her.

The head of security gave Sandy the rest of the day off—all forty-five minutes of it—so Sandy made her way back to the con hotel. For once, there was no line at the elevators going up to the rooms. She punched the Up button and stood waiting, her head bent down, not really looking at anything but her shoes.

Check that. Her black combat boots. Comfortable, but probably not sexy enough for a blue-furred alien bombshell.

She never heard anyone walk up behind her. She didn't even know someone was there until she felt them invade her personal space.

She tensed. Today was definitely *not* the day to violate the con's harassment policy. Not with this cosplayer.

"There you are," said a sexy, silky voice right next to Sandy's ear. "You make a very convincing cop, I have to say."

Sandy looked up and saw a reflection of gorgeous blue fur in the shiny surface of the elevator doors.

She turned around. The two of them were the only ones waiting for an elevator. Bianca's friend was nowhere in sight.

Sandy smiled up at the first real furry she'd ever known. "Well, I had to stay in character," she said. "It *is* Cosplay Day."

"For you. For me, it's a vacation day."

"Vacation?"

Bianca grinned "Where else can I go on your planet when I'm on vacation?"

True. An anime con would be about the only place—outside of a furry convention—where a six-foot tall, blue-eyed, blue-eared, blue-furred alien with a tail wouldn't seem out of place.

Bianca's grin widened. "And I have to say, I do like your planet. You have the most interesting people here."

The elevator doors opened. Six con attendees got off, five of them cosplayers. No one gave Bianca a second glance.

As soon as they got on the elevator—by themselves—Bianca pressed the "close doors" button and wrapped Sandy in a fierce hug. The next thing Sandy knew, Bianca was kissing the stuffing out of her.

"Wow," Sandy said when their lips parted. "That was possibly the best kiss of my life."

"I'm not being too aggressive?" Bianca asked.

Was she kidding? "I've been thinking about doing exactly that ever since we met," Sandy said.

"Good to know."

Bianca kissed her again, although not quite as deeply this time.

"Most humans aren't as open to us as we are to them," she said when the kiss was over.

"Well, I'm not exactly a normal girl." Or so Sandy'd been told by most of the girls she'd dated. "I do have one question, though."

Bianca laughed. "Only one?"

"Well, for now." She actually had lots of questions, but she really needed the answer to this one now. "Who was that guy anyway? And why was he going to shoot you?"

Bianca stroked the back of Sandy's head. It felt more than nice.

"We forgot to put in our travel permits," she said. "Last minute details, and we just forgot. Our names came up on the list."

"The list? Like a no-fly list?"

"More like a traffic fine list. Most of the time no one tries to enforce those things until you put it for the next trip, but he's a trainee looking to make a name for himself."

"You can get killed for that?" Talk about harsh!

"Are you kidding? We're a lot tougher than we look." Bianca's grin faded a bit. "You're not. I'm glad you didn't get hurt."

Sandy decided not to dwell on that.

"Are you going to get in trouble?" she asked. What she really wanted to know was whether Bianca was going to have to cut her vacation short.

"I doubt it. We had a little chat." Bianca's expression took on a decidedly wicked look. "He'd never live it down if word got out he was defeated by a human with a toy gun. We took care of the paperwork and paid our fine, so no one else is going to come after us."

The elevator stopped on the fourteenth floor and a middle-aged couple got on.

The couple clearly weren't con-goers. They were dressed in business casual, and neither of them had con badges or wristbands.

Sandy smiled at them and took half a step away from Bianca. Don't freak the normals was a good rule of thumb the con encouraged their volunteers to follow.

The woman gave Bianca and Sandy a look that would have frozen molten lava.

"I've had all my shots," Bianca said to the couple. "And I promise not to bite."

Sandy stifled a laugh. She wished she could think of things like that to say in the moment, instead of an hour or so later.

The couple spent the short trip steadfastly *not* looking at Bianca. They got out on the eighteenth floor. Sandy glanced up at Bianca, who was gazing down at her with a soft smile on her not-so-human face.

"So," Sandy said, drawing out the word. "What floor do you need?"

Bianca hadn't pressed any of the buttons on the elevator control panel when she'd gotten on the elevator. Sandy'd barely had time to press the button for her room on the twentieth floor.

Bianca touched her finger against Sandy's chin, and time slowed down again. The same marvelous feeling tingled through her chin and down her spine to lodge in a totally wonderful place.

"Who said I'm staying here?" she asked.

———

Much later—much, *much* later, when they got back to Sandy's room thanks to Bianca's nifty teleportation ability, not to mention her way of stretching time, Sandy realized that she'd finally done something her mom had been after her to do for years.

She'd made a friend at the con.

Not exactly the type of friend her mom hoped she'd settle down with, but definitely a nice friend.

She smiled at Bianca and giggled.

"What?" Bianca said, flicking Sandy's nose with the tip of her tail, which did, in fact, show up for more than just stress.

"I was just wondering what my mom would say if I introduced you," Sandy said.

Bianca's ears twitched. "How would you explain me?"

How could she explain any of what happened today?

Yeah, mom? Today I tackled an interstellar traffic cop and knocked his ray-gun away before he could shoot two really tall blue aliens and maybe a bunch of other people. Oh, and by the way, one of the aliens is my girlfriend now. I think I'm in love with her tail. And her ears.

"On second thought, maybe not," Sandy said.

At least not for now. But maybe someday.

Bianca had told Sandy that she visited Earth a *lot*. "Got hooked on the cons," she'd said. "They're actually kind of fun."

The two of them had already made plans to meet up at a big anime con in Los Angeles next month.

And after that?

Who knew? There was always a con going on somewhere.

Which meant…

"So…" Sandy touched the tip of her finger to the soft skin on Bianca's chin as she got a sudden thought. "You like vacationing on Earth for the cons. Is there anything on your planet I could go to?"

Bianca gave her a bemused look. "You'd need a costume."

"Of course."

"And you'd have to give yourself over to the part."

Sandy grinned. "Like today, you mean?"

Bianca grinned back. "We could definitely work on it."

"Awesome!"

That's all Sandy had ever really wanted anyway—a girlfriend to go to cons with.

So what if she was a blue-furred, blue-eared, blue-eyed alien?

The type of cons they both liked going to—on Earth or somewhere else—they'd fit in just fine.

PEPPER PRETORIOUS SAVES THE DAY

DAYLE A. DERMATIS

Professional fiction writer Dayle A. Dermatis always writes great stories, but also is a guest editor in our Fiction River *series. Under numbers of names, she has published more stories than I think she can count.*

In this really original and crazy young-adult story, Dayle introduces us to Pepper, one of the most original and interesting third-graders I would ever hope to meet. Oh, and there are aliens, too.

———

Penelope Pretorious, known as Pepper to everyone (and Peepee, only once, by a classmate who would never do *that* again), danced quietly in the back of her third-grade classroom. She was one of the Active children, the kind formerly punished for not being able to sit still in their seats before childhood educators figured out that some children simply needed to be able to move around. The deal was, an Active child could go to the back of the room where the padded mats were and work off their excess energy as they needed to, so long as they kept quiet, learned the lessons the teacher was teaching, and didn't disturb other children. For Pepper, that was dancing.

Her father was South African and her mother Chinese, and her complexion was similar to the reddish clay earth outside the dome and her hair was shiny-black and straight. She was of an average build for an eight-year-old, and perhaps slightly more graceful when she was paying attention, which wasn't always.

Pepper was actually the smartest child in her third-grade class, currently the only third-grade class in the domed colony of Danu on the fourth planet in orbit around the star Niamh, a G V star in the May 14015 system. (Pepper didn't entirely understand how all those words fit together, but they were Important, because every child learned to recite them.)

Well, she was the smartest human. The only student who

could give her a run for her money was Croxel, which wasn't exactly his real name but humans couldn't exactly pronounce the real names of the V'xanns, who were aliens.

V'xanns had four arms and were very, very skinny. Their multiple armlike appendages moved like the tentacles on jellyfish Pepper had seen in videos, languid and floating, although they could stiffen them to pick things up or write or whatever. Their skin was a muted purple that shaded from a light grey-lavender on the youngest to stormy amethyst on the oldest ones. Their hair was a short, fine layer that wafted in the air. (Pepper liked that word, *wafted*.)

Otherwise, they were sort of human-sized and shaped. The only other big difference was their voices.

Older V'xanns could sound like two or three or more people speaking at once. Because this was confusing and alarming to humans, they had learned to mute the extra levels so they could live and work alongside humans.

There was another colony on the other side of the planet, but they didn't count, at least not to Pepper, when it came to the question of the smartest kid in third grade. The other colony was almost as theoretical as Earth to Pepper.

Pepper looked forward to fourth grade (which was *forever* away), when her class would get a field trip to the other colony. The V'xanns had some way of getting there easily. As Pepper understood it, they sort of flew. She guessed it had something to do with their really long limbs.

Pepper danced in the back of the classroom, listening to Ms. Sjöberg talk about fractions, which Pepper already understood, and wished she had floaty limbs like the V'xann's, because she couldn't quite get her arms to move the way she wanted to.

It was terribly important that she did.

Someone had decided that there were finally enough children in all the grades in the school to put on a talent show.

It wasn't supposed to be a competition, but she wished it

could be. Being the best in the show was as important to her as being the smartest kid in third grade, thank you very much.

Pepper liked being the best at things. It made her feel wiggly and smiley inside when her parents or her teacher told her she'd done well.

She paused in her practice dancing to look at the fractions problem the teacher had put on the board, solved it in her head, and nodded in satisfaction when the teacher confirmed her mental calculation. Then she went back to dancing.

There were no dancing teachers on the planet, which Pepper thought was terribly unfair, even though her parents had explained to her that the people in charge back on Earth thought it best that the colony be populated by scientists. She found instructional vid-recs of dancing—there were vid-recs of just about everything, and her parents said that art was still very important—and did her best to follow the movements.

Her best, she had decided, was very good.

Her friends Douglas and Mikhaila had asked her to do something with them for the talent show, but she'd declined. They were her friends, but they weren't as good as she was. They were almost as smart, true, but they were clumsy when it came to dancing, and the three of them couldn't agree on something to do together anyway.

The two of them were teaming up to do something, though, but Pepper wasn't worried about the competition.

Didn't matter that there were kids from higher grades in the show, either. She was a little worried about the various V'xann students, because they might choose to dance, too, so she practiced even harder.

Pepper was determined to be the best.

———

Dome meetings were held in public spaces, because of things

like "human contact" and "benefits of getting outdoors," which Pepper didn't understand. They weren't outdoors; they were under the dome, which was a big vidscreen that mimicked the Earth sky, right down to blue skies, clouds (although it never rained, obviously), and sunshine. At night, however, the dome's vidscreen went clear so everyone could see the stars.

The stars looked different than they did when viewed from Earth, apparently.

The public space for the dome meeting was a big park. Adults chatted while they waited for the meeting to start. When it did, they'd hear the boring stuff through their earjacks.

The ground was a spongy green material that was supposed to be like grass on Earth, but Pepper had never seen grass. She liked the way this ground felt under her feet, especially when she leapt into the air and came down again.

Other kids played, or watched a vid-rec, but Pepper had to practice. The show was one week away, which was a long time, but she needed all the practice she could get.

She didn't do her actual routine, because she wanted people to experience the whole thing at the show. She did little parts of it, the hardest ones, over and over, trying to get them right. She leapt and twirled and dipped, and waved her arms as much like the V'xanns' graceful movements as she could. Sometimes she paused, cocked her head, and looked at her imaginary audience.

Always, she smiled.

Smiling made people happy.

During one of her pauses, she saw that her teacher, Ms. Sjöberg, had come over to talk to her parents. That probably meant Ms. Sjöberg was saying something nice about her.

Pepper didn't mean to listen, not really, even though she liked to hear people say nice things about her. But she wasn't supposed to go too far away from her parents, so it wasn't really her fault if she overheard something.

"If Pepper plays her cards right, she could steal the show," Ms. Sjöberg said.

Pepper's father laughed, and her mother said, "I don't doubt that."

Pepper didn't know what cards had to do with dancing, nor why she would ever want to steal the show when she wanted her dance to be the *highlight* of said show, the performance everyone would be talking about afterwards.

Adults were weird sometimes. So were aliens. But it was rude to say it about aliens.

————

The evening of the talent show, Pepper was more nervous than she was before a spelling bee. She was never nervous before spelling bees, because she always won them.

She was, after all, the smartest child in her class.

She had a fair sense of how talented the other children in her class were, but she had less of an idea about the other grades. Kindergarten through second grade were unlikely to produce any major upsets.

The older children in fourth, fifth, and sixth grades, though...

She'd realized she had no idea about them.

That made her nervous.

"Just do your best, Pepper," her mother said, hugging her. "That's all we ask for."

Of course she was going to do her best. Adults were weird.

Well, if her teacher and her parents were correct, she was somehow going to steal the show. She still wasn't clear on that, but she'd made it a secondary goal to being the very best, just in case it turned out to be important.

A stage had been set up in the park where the community meetings were held, with many, many chairs, and those in the back could watch on their vids if they couldn't see the stage. Parents were in the front rows. Performers sat along the back of the stage.

Pepper sat politely during the younger children's performances. There was some singing, some poem recitation (with prompts from the wings), and even some dancing, but as expected, they weren't even close to her level of talent.

Croxel sat next to her. Pepper noticed he seemed nervous, too. Noticing that made her feel strange. It made her feel good, but then she felt bad for feeling good, as if she wasn't supposed to.

Inspired by something they'd seen on an old vid-rec, Pepper's friends Douglas and Mikhaila shouted jokes at each other while doing something they called juggling, which seemed to consist of throwing things at each other and trying to catch them.

Pepper laughed when the audience did, even though she didn't find the jokes funny. Like the one where Douglas said "a bunch of cows" and Mikhaila said "a herd," which was correct, but then Douglas protested that of course he'd heard of cows. Pepper knew "herd" and "heard" were two different words, and she knew Douglas and Mikhaila did, too. It made no sense.

Finally it was Pepper's turn. She stood up, took a deep breath, and danced out into the middle of the stage.

She pivoted and twirled, she dipped and leapt, she did her best to *waft*. She smiled and smiled. Her dance was, she knew deep down where it counted, beautiful. When the music came to an end, she bowed low as a hearty applause washed over her, and she was sure it was the loudest applause so far, and she knew, as she straightened and looked out into the rows of people—her parents, her friends' parents, teachers, and strangers, human and alien alike—that she had not only done her best, but she had been the best of all so far.

And would be the best of all at the end.

She sailed back to her seat, filled with pride, passing Croxel on the way.

He stood on the stage along with six other V'xanns, one from their third-grade class, the others probably from higher grades, given their size. They all were still shades of pale lavender-grey, though, so Pepper knew they weren't adults.

They arranged themselves in a semicircle, all facing the audience. Between them, Pepper could see down into the first row, and saw her mother and father smiling proudly at her.

Then the V'xanns began to sing as one.

Pepper was startled. She was used to talking to Croxel and the other V'xanns in her class, with their singular voices. Joined together, the voices sounded like what an adult V'xann's did if they weren't changing it to sound better to human ears.

She had heard an unmodulated adult V'xann speak a few times, but never sing. This must be what that sounded like.

The song was kind of spooky, but also kind of fascinating. Pepper felt like something was tickling her skin, but from the inside.

At first she kind of liked it, and moved her arms to the music. (She wanted to get up and dance, but she knew this wasn't like being in the classroom, and if she wanted to dance, she'd have to leave.)

Then she realized that if the music made her feel good, it might be making other people feel good, and they might decide the song was better than her dance. Pepper's lower lip crept out, just a tiny bit, and she frowned.

As the song got louder, she decided she *didn't* like the way it made her feel. Her tummy and her head felt funny.

Pepper heard a strange, low murmur and realized it was coming from the audience. She twisted in her seat, rising to her knees on the padding to see over the V'xann children on stage.

The V'xanns in the audience were waving their many arms and making the noise, which didn't sound happy.

As she watched and listened, their unhappy noises got louder, and they were waving their arms up and down in what she knew meant in alien-speak, "Stop." They were doing it quickly, like they were agitated.

She whipped her head back to the stage. The V'xann children clearly saw and heard their adults, but they ignored them.

Pepper held her breath. You never ignored what adults told you. That would just get you into trouble. You couldn't be the best if you were in trouble.

Croxel and his friends were going to be in so much trouble.

The song got louder, and the tickling feeling got stronger, and Croxel's parents, sitting in the front row, leapt up on their tentacle-y legs. All the V'xanns were getting up, and making louder noises, as if to drown out the children on stage.

Then, suddenly, there was a loud POP! and everything went dark for a moment.

Pepper thought she was going to throw up, and she pressed her lips together. That would be just too embarrassing.

Then the lights came back on, and she realized why her tummy felt so funny. She grabbed onto her seat because she felt as if she would float away.

The stage was no longer in the park.

The stage was no longer in the dome.

They somehow hovered over the dome, and they shouldn't be able to breathe—every child, down to kindergarten, knew the air outside the dome wasn't the right kind of air—but there was some kind of bubble around them.

All at once, Pepper understood.

This was what her parents and teacher had meant by "stealing the show."

They'd been wrong, though: Pepper hadn't been the one to do it.

The V'xanns had.

And Pepper was *furious*.

This. Was. Not. FAIR!

They had lied to her. There was no way she could've stolen the show because she didn't have the teleporting song the V'xanns did.

There was no way she could have been best, no matter how hard she practiced.

Pepper never in her life had had a temper tantrum, but there were no adults here now, only the other children sitting along the back of the stage (some of them were crying), and she had never felt such rage and unfairness and helplessness.

She sucked in a deep breath and screamed. It was loud and it was shrill and piercing, and the kids who were crying stopped, their mouths open, and even the V'xanns in the middle of the stage stopped singing.

Finally.

Pepper screamed until she ran out of breath, and then she sucked in more air and screamed again, stamping her feet on the ground. It was in the middle of that scream that she heard another POP! and everything went dark again.

She was so startled, her scream cut off abruptly.

When the light returned, they were back in the park, and it seemed like lots of people were screaming or crying and running around, and the humans were shouting and the V'xanns were wafting frantically.

Pepper, frustrated, kicked her chair and started to sob, very quietly.

———

The next day, Ms. Sjöberg sat everyone down—even the Active kids had to sit still and listen—and explained that the V'xanns hadn't been honest about how far their abilities went; they hadn't explained that they could transport whole stages and maybe even more. So for now, until they all spent a long time talking to each other, the V'xanns were being asked to stay away from humans.

Then she thanked everyone for being very brave at the talent show, and she smiled at Pepper and said that Pepper should be especially thanked because her screaming had stopped the adolescent V'xanns from singing, which had allowed the adults in the dome to take over and teleport the stage back inside to the park.

Pepper, Ms. Sjöberg said, had saved the day.

Well. *That* made no sense, either. How did you save a day? When the sun set, the day ended. You couldn't keep it and have it the next day. Maybe she'd saved the show, but the whole day?

Pepper didn't say anything about it to Ms. Sjöberg, however, because whatever Ms. Sjöberg was talking about, it was clear she thought Pepper had done a good job.

Plus, the way she was singling Pepper out and having the other children clap, it was clear Pepper had done the *best* job.

Which meant Pepper had been the best at the talent show.

And with Croxel gone, Pepper was *definitely* the smartest child in the whole third grade in the domed colony of Danu.

With that settled, Pepper went to the back of the classroom and danced.

HERO OF FIRE LIFE

MICHAEL WARREN LUCAS

Michael Warren Lucas might have one of the most twisted and innovative minds in fiction that I have had the pleasure to read. He has published over thirty books in all sorts of areas, from science fiction to fantasy to thrillers to non-fiction and just about everywhere between.

For this collection, Michael gave us a very, very strange take on aliens and superheroes. Trust me, you've never read anything like this one before.

———

So I'm walking down Mack Avenue—not the good parts, but down by Grand Boulevard where the old nineteenth-century mansions are either crumbling or braced with twisted two-by-fours and busted breezeblock. The best looking ones are the mental health group homes. Those places have to take care of their houses, or the State stomps in and shuts 'em right down. Other houses, folks just make do. There's a lot of busted-out windows with trash bags taped over them. But they swept up the glass, so it's all good.

It's the first fake spring day and the snow's still on the ground, steaming in the sunlight and keeping last fall's leaves frozen so they can't throw up the mold stink, so the air's still winter-fresh. It's warm enough I'm in a T-shirt so the sun can thaw my bones.

Got a warm coat over my shoulder, though. The weather was gonna turn on us real soon. Probably with a blizzard. The warmth lured me outdoors and set me walking, and I'm probably gonna freeze for it, but I couldn't resist.

I'm not the only one. Kids are playing basketball on the court behind the First Baptist, and some idiot's fired their smoker. Pork slow-cooking over seasoned applewood is one of those smells that tells you everything's gonna be just fine. Smoking takes *hours*, though. The chef will finish up tonight huddled in his winter coat tonging ribs while snowflakes spatter the smoker and burn straight to steam.

The idiot's got the right idea.

The neighborhood's starting to poke up little green leaves of life. The storefront COGIC has its doors open for an airing. Someone's even rented the old billboard for an ad for a Wesley Snipes action comeback. Man, that guy can do one hell of a drop-dead crazy glare. Someone walks out of the liquor store a couple blocks up and stretches his arms to catch air that for once is not trying to kill him.

It's that kind of day when you know winter's really gonna get lost and you'll be able to open the door and air the place out. Maybe not now, but some day not too far off.

I've walked so much my feet are starting to hurt. Last summer I'd gone a hell of a lot further, all the way down to Eastern Market, but winter keeps you close to home. Forget the ice, just the slush will do you in. Snow-march cardio ain't distance cardio. I got my boots on, cause the sidewalks are rivers of melt and lots of places the curb's overflowing cause the drains ain't been cleaned since Clinton. My feet are dry, but the instep isn't made for this kind of hike.

Younger me would have gone right on, but I'm just old enough to start to figure out that my feet are gonna blame me tomorrow. I ain't old. Not yet. But I'm at the top of that hill looking down and I can see how the arthritis is gonna get bad.

And the weather was gonna pull a knife any time.

Plus, there's that new history series on Netflix.

So I turn around, and the hero's right there. I damned near jumped out of my skin.

I mean, he had to be a hero, right? Wearing neon blue long underwear, and stupid tight bright-yellow Jockeys over them. And that's the first thing that told me something was wrong, cause those undies were so damn tight his timbits and tonker ought to be poking out—no, I don't go staring at people's junk, but those undies were bright yellow and he was taller'n me, right? I mean, his chest was right at eye level and if I wore undies like that I'd squeak so hard they'd call an ambulance. Made my eyes water.

I ain't never seen a chest so wide—but smooth, you know? The shirt looked tight, but I'm not sure what it was tight *over*. Too flat for muscle.

He got this chin you could plow asphalt with, and bright eyes. No, not like he's interested—they was literally lit up. From inside. Not bright like LEDs, just enough to show you something ain't right.

Anyway, he looks at me and says, "Greetings, Living Fire Person Citizen."

Maybe he's from one of them group homes. "Hey. Howya doing?" I stepped aside into the muddy grass let him pass. You always give crazy the right of way, if you like going home again.

His face was too pink. I thought it was maybe crazy meds that made him that way, that made his skin too smooth. A big chest like that, this time of day, man ought to have a five-o-clock shadow.

He says, "Could you direct me to the nearest bank robbery?"

Now, I've talked to a lot of the crazies. Met a guy once, thought he was Jesus. You shoulda seen the fight he had with the woman cross the street what thought she was Buddha. But I'd never seen no one what thought they were a comic book superhero. And not one of the angsty new ones, but a proper hero. Like I grew up with.

It'd explain the underwear.

"Where you from, mister?" I says.

"I come from the Doomed Planet Cryptic." He sounded like a proper hero, too, like one of those old scratched-up 50s serials they showed on TV when I was a kid. "I'm here to show the Fire Life the meaning of Truth and Justice."

I couldn't help smiling. If you got to be crazy, might as well be one of the good guys, am I right? "I don't know any bank robberies round here, sorry."

He frowned—no, that ain't right. He was smiling, then he was frowning, but his face didn't go from one to the other. It didn't bother to change, it just *was*. Like on a computer, you know? I thought I'd blinked, at first.

"Then perhaps a fire," he says.

A truck grumbled past, right through this pool of melt and throwing up trashy water. Children shouted cheerful smack talk and a basketball thomped wet but regular on soggy black-top. There's all these folks grabbing all the spring they can steal, and this guy's beginning to worry me. "I don't hear any sirens. Listen, maybe you ought to head home?"

"We have studied the Fire Life People's records," the hero says. "Mastering your language and culture demanded over fifty of your Fire Life Years. I cannot return home from your bizarre and ridiculous world without achieving your respect. You must have a kitten up a tree."

The trees ain't even started to bloom. Winter gales took all the weak branches. "Do you see any kittens?"

"Kidnapping?"

"There you go!" I'm getting tired of the gag. "I'm sure some-one's been kidnapped. I bet your caregiver could tell you exactly who."

"My support team is in high orbit. They know nothing of fire-life kidnappers."

I admit it. I kind of get a kick out of some of the crazies, you know? They think their bullshit through. "What is this 'fire life' you keep talking about?"

"Your whole planet!" the hero says. "Every life here. You propel your lives by burning your body in unadulterated oxygen. No other world is so insane as to design their biome in such a manner. We needed much research to create probes that would withstand your atmosphere, and until the Fire Suit—" He claps his hand to his chest. "The pinnacle of our technology —none could visit."

It's the way his hand hit his chest that told me something was wrong.

The crazies give a convincing line. Sometimes, part of you kinda believes them.

But no matter how crazy you are, your chest don't clank when you hit it with your bare hand. I swear, it clanked. Not like armor, either. Not hollow. Like when you hit an engine block with an iron bar.

My guts kind of went liquid right then. Lucky I didn't ruin my pants.

I still thought he was a crazy. But a crazy strong enough to carry all that metal—no, it didn't make no sense. He had that smile, that Chin of Doom.

Crazies ain't that pretty.

Heck, movie stars ain't that pretty.

Whatever this guy was, from the Doomed Planet Whatever, he wasn't no normal crazy.

"I thought it best to start small," he says—no, he *proclaims*, like one of those preachers that rip off the poor folks. "Perhaps the Fire Life has solved these lesser problems. Take me to your Hitler."

I looked around for anyone who might help, but the kids are all hooting at their b-ball game and the old ladies chatting around the stoop'll just duck back inside if the trouble starts, and the cars ain't gonna stop nohow. I'm trying to buy some thinking time so I says, "Hitler?"

"Your records show that fighting through an army and punching a Hitler is the standard method of achieving recognition and honor among Fire Life." His chin somehow thrusts out even more. "I shall be known among the whole of the pancosmos as the one who first dared to dare the Fire Life!"

Yeah, the way he clanked worried me, but my brain was starting to kick in. The smart part, what insisted he was a crazy, was getting drowned out by the sensible part that said maybe this guy was legit. I mean, he even looked like he was out of a comic book, one of the old ones Dad kept from when he was a kid, where they had big lines and only a few colors of ink. That face was a pink that I ain't seen on *nothing* living. A chest that big ought to have all kinds of muscles showing up through the shirt.

And the undies.

No way any man could wear undies *that* tight.

"Oh, right," I says. "Hitlers." I thought of naming some politicians, you know the ones, but figured that'd just go horrible wrong. "You know we defeated Hitler most of a century ago, right? We're okay. Don't need no heroes no more."

"Fire Life always needs heroes," he says. "Your records say so, over and over again. He almost destroys you, and is defeated. Take me to your Hitler."

"Look." I caught myself licking my lips. Not a good look, and besides, in this weather they'll just chap the hell up. "You said you took many years to translate those records. That ain't what we're like no more. Our heroes are quiet now. Doctors and philanthropizers. Stuff like that."

The way the hero's head turns on his neck isn't right. When a person looks around, their skin moves. His just didn't.

Then his head just...kept turning.

I'm looking at the back of his head. He doesn't have hair, it's like, all plastic.

My guts had gone all soft before, but now they're hard. I've got a brick in my guts and it's gonna need more than a prune to get rid of.

"Aha!" The hero shouts so loud I jump. The steady thomp-

thomp-thomp of the b-ball goes all *thompthompthud* and stops, and them kids raise their own shouts.

The hero turns his head back to me, which eases my innards a little but not near enough, and raises his hand. "If you have defeated your Hitlers," he says, "then who does this Fire Life fight?"

He's pointing at the movie billboard, where Wesley Snipes glares all mean and ready to pound someone's face. There's even fire behind him.

I can't help take half a step back. The hero's frown is bigger now, and his eyebrows have turned way too far down into a scowl. People can't scowl that far, and I should know. My Aunt Rosa was a champion scowler.

"There are Hitlers," he says. "They always come back. Who are you? Are you one of those that saved Hitler's brain?"

I raise my hands up, but keep 'em open. You don't show a fist down here, not less you plan to use it. "It's a story! We tell that story to everyone, over and over again. It's so if a Hitler shows, we know to fight him. That's how you beat them, you stomp them early."

"A story?" He sounds right pissed now. "You lie about your Hitlers?"

I make myself swallow. "It's teaching for the young. For new, new Fire Life. We burn up, right?" Someone's walking up the street behind the hero, but they're still like a block and a half away and I don't know how I could explain this quick enough so they'd help. I mean this hero, whatever he is, showed up ready to punch an army so he could deck Hitler. "We burn ourselves to death, and the new Fire Life need to know of the danger for when Hitlers come again."

The hero eyes me like one of those young men lounging round street corners at three in the morning. "You are among the wholesome citizenry of the Fire Life people."

I nod, quick as I can.

His chest inflates a good six inches, and he gives this sigh that blows my hair back hard. "Then you speak the truth. There is no enemy for me to fight to gain your respect."

I nod. "That's right. We don't need heroes any more. We done saved ourselves. It's all the Internet and philanthophizers now."

The hero's head does one slow turn, full around. My eyes want to squeeze back into my head just watching.

"Then I cannot do this as I hoped," the hero says.

Between one breath and the next, he's just...gone.

I kind of sag right there. My heart's threatening to run off, and suddenly I'm right cold. The fake spring hasn't gone away, but my shirt's soaked through with sweat and if'n I don't get my coat on I'm gonna catch a chill. I can't miss work no more.

And I'm right tired. Time enough to chew all this over once I'm home.

Or, maybe, someone'll notice that I've lost what brains I had and move me down to one of those group homes permanent-like. That's the kind of things us wacked-out oxygen breathers do, I guess.

I'm barely a hundred feet down the street, just across from the open doors of the COGIC, when a great big voice bellows behind me. "ATTENTION!"

There's a huge black-and-jewel metal spider in the middle of Mack Avenue. Its body fills the turn lane, and all them legs block all the traffic going either way. Trucks skid and the cars are a big tangle of metal straightaway, but the spider doesn't even wobble.

I clap my hands over my ears and try to stuff that sickening dread back down.

"Attention!" the spider trumpets. "I am the Mightiest Hitler. Your lives are mine. Your world is mine."

Then—swear to God—it starts growing.

Sore feet or no, tired or no, I started running.

Something gave a big *thomp* behind me, and I feel all this heat at my back.

Something done blew up.

I spare a thought for the kids playing basketball. Hope they're smart enough to run. Then I tuck my elbows into my sides and pound down melt-covered sidewalks.

If I can run far enough, I'll be fine.

See, right when we've lost everything, a hero's coming to save us.

BUSHTITS GONE WILD

STEPHANIE WRITT

Stephanie Writt is a regular contributor to Pulphouse Fiction Magazine *and the* Fiction River *series. She always writes characters you can't soon forget, all with attitude and a wonderful, wonderful voice.*

In this original story, she uses that voice and an original character to show us some truly original aliens in a way that will keep you on the edge of your seat while reading. And the title does make sense once you read the story, I promise.

———

To say I moved to Arizona for the women is about as accurate as saying I've sold insurance for twenty-nine years because I like talking to people.

I did expect a little more variety than the sea of cotton candy heads adorned in freshly puffy-painted sweatshirts that spelled out variations on the theme "Best Grandma Ever" with an army of stick figures representing the amount of dick fucking they did before they realized that they preferred to eat pussy.

By the way, I'm an over-sixty lesbian. No kids. Few boundaries. And I have a cat.

Currently partner-less in a brand new city.

Which was why I was wading through the sickeningly sweet crowd of high-pitched over-pleasant chatter, way too falsely excited about life, in the hopes of finding someone my own age that didn't rely on a walker or have a lifetime subscription to Crochet World magazine.

We all had our priorities, and mine was to find the sane old people in that desperate mass of "mature" (my left tit) bodies that hovered in small groups across the blindingly reflective wooden dance floor of the Sedona Community Center.

The high ceilinged expanse was elegantly adorned with a scattering of round tables, clothed in the blazing bright rainbow of tru-tone colors that lay at the heart of the southwestern design style. Atop each, an additional array of eye assaulting orange and indigo colored Fiestaware plates held high-end finger foods of such quality as bologna and America cheese.

Hello, sarcasm.

Well dear god, they either needed to mix old lady lesbian night with the gathering of the gray-haired gays that wished they could still wear hot pants. Or beg one of them with any sort of style (all of them, likely) to take mercy upon our souls and ban the jello-molds.

This was not 1973.

Thank. Fucking. Christ.

So.

I politely ignored all the women who approached me or attempted to stop my desperate wanderings with pickup lines that ranged from empty chatter to more empty chatter. About shit I avoided at most costs. Like children. And more children. And anything involving a glue gun.

I finally spotted a head of hair that was perm-free, dye-free, and framed a face with eyes of a genuine sparkle though she wasn't smiling. She was in deep conversation with a small gathering of other like-haired women.

None of them looked a part of the "I've fallen and can't get up" category. All tanned, with muscle definition beneath their browned or browner skin. Their clothing ranged from simple Eddie Bauer all the way to Frankensteined together hippie couture.

I felt like a giddy school girl when I saw one of them was wearing boots. Honest to god, worn hiking boots. Scuffed and coated in the red dust of the desert into foot hugging perfection.

I think I fell in love with her because of her boots.

But that is not what this story is about.

I'm giving a preliminary, so when I call her after my total reality goes to total shit you've got some background on her.

Well, I guess more on me. But, there it is.

The first word I heard uttered in the group was "bushtits" and though I had never heard those two words put together in quite that way, I thought I might have missed a sizzling joke and these were my kinda ladies.

Nope.

They were birders, I later learned. Bird lovers. Bushtit was a type of bird.

But I wouldn't learn that for almost another twenty-four hours. A little late for what came next.

Boot-gal shook her shoulder length salt & pepper at me in warning halfway through my dropping of a scandalous joke into the group as an ice-breaker.

Ice-shattered into a world filled with crickets and loose jaws.

"Well fuck," I said and gave up.

Boot-gal caught up to me in the parking lot with a gentle slide on the gravel and a hand on the tailgate of my Tacoma. She wasn't out of breath from her jog and my estimation of her shot up a couple pegs. I 5Ked it every other morning before the sun was high enough to bake out my lungs. Maybe she did the same.

She dropped a business card in my palm and 15 mins later—

No, we weren't kissing, but I'd sure wanted to. She didn't smile needlessly and I wanted to thank her lips for that.

—15 mins later I was driving away with one hand on the steering wheel and the other fingering the card she gave me with deep consideration.

Bethany Brown. Semi-retired, on-call veterinarian.

And she made house calls.

I made plans to talk to Jeff, my white-bellied tabby, about getting a stuck hairball or something in the next couple of days so I had at least a mildly legitimate reason to call Bethany Brown.

Bethany Brown. With her perfect boots and hidden smile.

Unfortunately, when I did call her she was most truly and desperately needed.

————

I was closing the deal on a health policy the next day with a couple recommended to me by another client. My work bread and butter. It paid for my three-bedroom, two-bath adobe-pink palace complete with stone tiled everything, a patio firepit and enough windows to create a cyclone through the house if the mostly stagnant air decided to stir itself into something greater than a heating blanket.

Laptop whirling on my bare thighs, I spotted Jeff through the sliding glass door just past my toes, lounging in the shade beneath the waist-high dividing wall that surrounded the patio outside.

A feeble attempt at keeping out the more dangerous of ground skittering creatures, I loved to perch on it at night, legs out, and stare up at the freeway of stars that streaked my new sky. Still in shorts and a tank top. The air cooling at piss-frenzy speed, but the adobe clay of the wall warming my buns and hands with the heat captured in the day.

Fat, lazy and perfectly content with the emptiness of his life, Jeff was my beloved companion that asked nothing of me except unending food and pets whenever he demanded it. It was a small price to pay for the warmth he gave my feet when I was already sweating in the night. Or the gift of suffocation when he slid down my chest and onto my neck, turning into the fur muff from hell.

It was a balanced relationship.

But in the middle of asking the husband for the wife's height and weight "as long as it won't get you in trouble" *insert laughter* Jeff made an eardrum splitting sound that no creature should ever be driven to utter.

All goofy-sweet sales lady dropped in a heart-splitting second.

Headphones and laptop were airborne off my body as I flew from the couch, my body passing through the open sliding glass door toward Jeff before I made a conscious decision to anything.

Blistering heat of the patio stones under foot registered just after the cyclone of birds that dove and sliced at Jeff.

And I mean sliced.

Blood sprays lined and spotted the wall ledge where Jeff huddled, as a flock of way too many tiny birds attacked him with beak and claw.

I snatched the broom from its lean against the wall of the house that assisted with my slightly manic need to tidy, and started swinging for the fences. Righty and southpaw, without care to injury to the damn birds.

Jeff's fur was already thickly wet in spots in just the few seconds from his first cry to my broom-bat thrashing.

I got in close enough to snatch him off the wall and tuck him under one arm, still swinging but a little more awkwardly with the other.

I sucked air with a zing as a tiny bird attack cut me open in a three-inch gash across my shoulder and down my back. Blood tickled down my chest. But I didn't bother with it.

I turned my back to the sliding glass door and backed up. Slowing. Swinging with a daily sweeper's practiced skill, (hell yeah after sixty years of it) and kept them off us until I could slam the door shut.

What in all the fucks?

There were nine birds. Nine.

How did I know?

Because they all hovered in place in a precise diamond formation at my eye level on the other side of the sliding glass.

They were tiny. About as long as my thumb and maybe as big around as kiwi. With two toothpick feathers for a tail.

The air stirred through the house just enough to breeze across my shoulder cut to make it burn.

And razor sharp claws?

My heart fluttered a second when one cheeped, turned its head, and cheeped again.

And wicked intelligence?

I don't know how I knew or why I thought the birds would, well, think. Instinct? Years of assessing people, voices, intent?

Another unconscious decision and Jeff was unceremoniously dropped on the couch and I was barefoot sprinting across the stone tiles that led from living room to dining to slam shut the second sliding glass door.

I even locked it.

Then dashed down the hall to slam shut each of the bedroom and bathroom windows, stone floor cooling my burned foot bottoms all the way.

The moisture left on the floor of the master bath from my mid-afternoon rinse off had me slipping and sliding, slowing me down before I slammed the final window shut just above the headboard of my bed.

I knelt on my mound of down pillows and heaved. A tightness in my chest more from nerves and fear than any heart issue.

In that split second I sucked air, I started the thought process to berate myself at my ridiculous fear.

They were birds.

They weren't going to know to look for other entrances to the house. To try to get in.

They hadn't even tried to get in. They had just hovered in front of the window. Menacingly.

How do tiny birds menace?

But just as that thought process started, it was slammed to a halt by the sound of a screech on glass.

I looked up and there they were.

The nine of them.

Hovering just outside the window, looking in at me in the same formation. Except for the one that rejoined the flock. A half-inch scrape in the glass from its claw.

I was suddenly glad I had been too busy to get my normal water intake for the day in or it would have outed itself all over my bed pillows.

Birds.

Right.

Now what in the fuck?

Jeff!

My foot-pads had dried in my bedding-scurry to the window, so I hauled in another cool-footed sprint to the living room without a slide—and gasped at my cat.

He was more blood-rust red than pumpkin orange. And he was panting. That stress pant, belly pulsing heave of an animal in way over its head.

And god dammit if one of those god damn birds wasn't in his god damn mouth.

"God dammit, Jeff!"

I've heard fear turns to anger, and fuck if I wasn't instantly blazing in rage at my dying cat.

I knelt down beside him, ignoring the pain in my knees from tissue pressing against hard stone (I'm healthy, not young). I didn't know where to touch him or not. He was a heaving pile of blood and fur with a mouth full of feathers. Finally I got my arms to work with enough focus to find and stroke his face. The bird there wasn't moving and I left it be. And I thought. Then I remembered.

Bethany Brown.

I hadn't realized I had memorized her phone number from

the truck ride home the night before and was dialing and shoving headphones on my ears simultaneously.

Not until I got a warbly "hello?" from a very confused man did I realize that my client was still on the phone.

How many minutes, seconds had passed?

Fuck if I knew or cared at that moment.

"I'll call you back," I unceremoniously spat into the phone, hung up and dialed Bethany Brown.

She picked up.

Relief.

I babbled out my situation between fucks and fuckings (I don't remember that, but I know myself enough to know my vocabulary becomes an f-bomb minefield in times of stress no matter the audience. I get shit done, but if small children are within earshot, they will come away with an education.)

I could hear the incredulousness in her voice from a half-crazed woman screaming about killer tiny birds, her near murdered cat, warning her to run for her life when she arrived.

Thank god I was poised to yank her inside the front door or she would have suffered more than the slice to her cheekbone standing there in shock as she did.

We tumbled to a pile with a bit of a slide on my welcome rug mock-up of a Jackson Pollock. It clashed with the entire state of Arizona, but I hadn't had a chance to swap out my previous decorative touches (though few) nor put those sticky things under it to keep it from becoming a carnival ride anytime you stepped upon it with any speed.

Breasts to breasts on the floor, our eyes met and she whispered, "Bushtits don't do that."

A whole slew of jokes and snarky remarks flooded my mind, but they were background noise to one thought.

"Jeff's on the couch."

I pushed her off me with quick force in the direction of Jeff and was beside her, kneeling against the couch again. She petted him with kind sounds and her left hand as her right probed his body. She made no outward reaction to anything she found.

She kept her low, kind voice when she said to me, still looking at Jeff, "I need any hand towels and washcloths you have or clean rags. And warm water."

Leaving her left hand to stroke him, her right unclipped her medical bag she carried and she started to rummage inside. It was one of those classic black house-call doctor's bags I'd only seen in movies. This one was precisely clean, shiny and I hoped filled with everything Jeff needed.

I didn't wait to see what she pulled out, but was at the stove warming a saucepan of water after near screaming at the faucet that released its precious liquid way too slowly. Then I was at the linen closets taking fistfuls of every small to medium cloth I could find, with full intent to cut up every 400-thread-count Egyptian cotton sheet I had if they were needed.

I had few companions in my life.

I am picky. And then I am loyal. And I admit, I get rather attached.

In this new desert land where everything seemed to want to kill you, including tiny cute little birds, Jeff was my only friend.

Nothing else really mattered at all in that moment.

Until the first crash.

I thought someone had taken a pickax to the sliding glass window.

Back down the hall to the living room, arms clutching cloth, I dropped my load beside Bethany Brown on the stone floor just as the second strike hit.

I would not have believed it if I hadn't seen it.

Bethany didn't believe it until the third strike and, pulling her eyes from prep-threading a needle (which I did not take as a good sign for Jeff), she saw it too.

It was those god damned birds.

Flying straight at the glass, slamming into it beak first.

Each hit, a chip of glass came away. They weren't "threading the needle" per se, but their chips were close together. Millimeters apart close together. Just a couple more chips and there would be a crack. And then a hole. And then we were in trouble.

But that was whole minutes away.

Jeff was still bleeding and Bethany's hands were flying.

She asked for the water and I grabbed it without checking. Potholder in case, I set it beside Bethany and commanded myself silent and out of her way. She moved with a confident competency that spoke to her decades of experience and also that if she fucking needed me, she would fucking say something.

My mind went to the next pressing issue at the fifth strike and glass chip.

What the fuck, birds?

And I saw the bird still held in Jeff's mouth.

Shiiiiiiiiit.

I knew enough about creatures that lived in communities that they get a little protective of one of their own in danger. I mean, these birds had gone all Marine "no one left behind," demonstrating abilities and a sentience that made no sense whatsoever. But whatever kind of bushtits these were, I bet they wanted their buddy back.

I gently began to pry Jeff's jaws apart with my own kind and soft, though vulgar, brand of cooing.

Stubborn fuck actually fought me.

Have the thread thin scars to prove it.

I'd never de-claw a cat, but by god I'd like to be able to ground him from them every once in a while.

Bethany finally held him while I popped his jaw open and pried out the ball of feathers and cat drool.

I snagged my own washcloth to wipe it down.

It was likely dead, but if I was going to give their friend back as a peace offering I didn't want to be a shit about it. Sorry about your friend. Splat. Stop attacking us now, ok?

Plus...well. *sigh* It was another living creature. And freakishly gifted or not, it had died. Been killed. It was nature and life, and I still could respectfully mourn.

I sniffed.

Awww, fuck.

But it was so damn tiny. It weighed nothing and felt as fragile as fuck.

Mostly cleaned, I stroked its feathers. So soft and perfect. Silk and fluff.

I gently petted the top of its head. Rubbed the pad of my fingertip between its four curled claw/toes like it was perching on my finger, though lying down. All spread, they were barely wider than my fingernail. Eyelashes for claws. Eyelashes that could cut glass...

A big old tear drop bumbled down my nose and splashed onto the birds face.

Well, good thing it's dead, because that would have drowned it for sure.

Strike.

Crack!

A couple of things happened all at once in that moment.

One: A foot long crack in my sliding glass door split off into frozen lightning.

Two: Bethany said, "I'm losing him," in her calm seriousness, her hands not slowing down one bit in their sewing and cleaning frenzy.

Three: The god damn bird in my hands woke up.

———

So, we all died. And this is me talking from heaven.

Oh, fuck no. Don't believe that shit for a second.

But the next part may be truly hard to believe.

Bethany and I have never told anyone about it because, well, we aren't stupid. Sedona is a small community and we can be involuntarily committed.

Fact.

So, Jeff is dying, killer birds are attacking, and the one inside the house was conscious and staring me down.

"What can I do?" I asked. I was looking at the bird though asking it of Bethany.

"Nothing," she said and kept moving.

The bird it was then.

And for some reason I will never be able to put to words I asked it the same question.

"What can I do?"

It didn't even do the bird tilt-tilt head thing when it looked at me. One side and then the other. Nope.

Straight, dead-on, into my eyes.

And then I felt a squeeze on my fingertip as those eyelash claws closed in with force. One, and then the other. And in a move I didn't recognize as reacting to any gravity laws I had been forced to endure, the bird was upright and perched on my finger.

Strike.

Crack!

Another foot-long crack. This one streaked right to the aluminum doorframe and ended where glass did.

Cheep!

The bird opened its beak and excreted a sound that had my eyes watering and froze all the birds in mid-flight. Because that was physically actual as well. (More sarcasm)

And then the bird on my finger turned inside-out.

No sarcasm here.

OK, stay with me on this one.

Its chest split open and a shimmering tendril of light and color came out.

Maybe a tentacle. A vine? Was it flora or fauna?

Whatever it was it was colored like the inside of an abalone shell and bright as the Las Vegas strip. It wrapped around my thumb.

A second wound out of the bird chest and wrapped around my wrist. Another and another in a mass that could not have fit inside that bird body, until tendril after tendril, vine after vine of beautiful light-creature-leg-things had wrapped around both my arms and hands, with one hooked just behind each of my knees. Nothing hurt. Nothing squeezed. And all feathers were gone.

Bethany continued to move over Jeff, which my heart ached in gratitude for. Because she did not even stutter her movements when she glanced over and saw my transforming companion.

She had a patient that needed her and fuck reality changing creatures.

Being head-over-heels for the woman solidified in that moment, though I'd address that later also.

At that point the creature looked like a strange flower with wrapping petals that pulsed with an extraordinarily lovely light. And from its center, where all the vines had sprung, a cloud of vapor that looked like translucent cotton fibers blew out of it and surrounded my face.

I held my breath as long as I could.

And then they were inside me and I was flying.

And then I was back in my body. And I knew, *knew*, that I had just had an extensive experience that I would be forever changed from. Fundamentally.

But I had no recollection of it.

Just a distant feeling, that word on the tip of the tongue, just past my fingertips, glass on the end of the table just an exhale from tumbling end-over-end in a golden orange juice arc of knowing.

But I did know. I knew a lot.

One thing I knew was that Jeff was not going to die.

Oh, no, that was not the creature magically saving him.

Nope, it was Bethany.

I knew in a place inside me that in those few moments from her words and now that she had successfully passed a critical point.

That knowing wasn't acute, like a word or idea. It had the breadth of a feeling. The expanse of a sky without bounds. Full and without ends, though not a cloud marked it. It was just huge and it just was.

And in that same kind of knowing, I knew this creature and its companions would no longer hurt us, because they now had a knowing about us, learning from me. And from me, a knowing of humans, this planet, the other life here.

Our issues and troubles.

The good, the bad and the fucked.

That we were not ready for them yet. But we were also worth waiting for.

And they got that all from me.

And the me before, being told that, would have f-bombed the world at that ridiculous notion. Judge the world on me? Jesus fuck and some Christ! Go talk to a nun or a child, or a kangaroo. A whale or an ant. They'd get a much better reading, or at least some varying perspective.

But apparently I was enough. And in that weird knowing, I understood. And was content with both their assessment and myself.

I mean, shit. That floating shit could have been half drug-aphrodisiac-alien bullshit.

But I knew, and I know, that it wasn't.

Like a flower folding up in the cool of night on fast-forward, all the vine tendrils of mega-sparkletown sucked back into itself until only a tiny bird stood perched on my finger.

It stared at me. Expecting.

This huge interaction and understanding happening between worlds and possibly time (I was not fully on the "knowing" about that, but I had gotten a whiff of it in there), and this was the parting of the ways. The moment of good-bye after a perspective shattering encounter that affected that whole of humanity and Earth itself.

I said, "OK."

And gave it a quick nod.

It cheeped once. Its own "OK" and then launched off my finger.

It flew toward the sliding glass door and cheeped again. This time the sound so fierce and poignant it hurt my eardrums. The call shattered glass, leaving a wall-less hole in the side of my house, opening it up to the universe outside.

Sunlight glittered off the wave of sea foam green glass shards that washed across my stone living room floor as the bird-alien joined its companions and, as a group, flew up into the perfect blue sky and out of sight, forever.

"Motherfucker!"

DOG PEOPLE

ROBERT J. MCCARTER

Robert J. McCarter has stories coming up in most of the next issues of Pulphouse Fiction Magazine. *He is a unique and true new voice just starting to appear on the scene.*

In this original story, Robert gives us a strange view into an alien family, but not in the way you might expect.

———

The wind was cold and sharp, driving crystalized snow into any uncovered body parts. My hands were going numb from taking pictures and my cheeks stinging from the snowy bombardment, but the view. My God, the view.

They call it the "Grand" Canyon for a reason and I think that reason is not just its depth, or its clear geological layers—the sandwiching of tan and reddish limestone and sandstone that reveals eons of history—or its many different moods and views depending on where and when you look from. I think they call it grand because of how all that looks with ten inches of snow at the top sticking to the trees and the rocks like huge globs of marshmallow and then slowly decreasing to a gentle dusting of confectionery sugar down on the Tonto Plateau above the inner gorge.

After a day of snow and the canyon mostly filled with clouds, only providing brief glimpses as if Mother Nature was doing an epic striptease, the canyon had finally revealed herself.

And the colors, the tans and reds and salmons were all intensified by the moisture and the low angle of the sun as it peeked through a gap in the thick clouds on the horizon.

My parents were bundled in their overpriced Patagonia parkas, purchased in some high-end store in LA just for this trip. They weren't looking at the awesome view but chatting away with another couple, standing on the rim about twenty yards away just in front of the dark brown bulk of the El Tovar lodge. This trip being another one of their visits to Arizona where I was getting my master's degree in business administration, and another one of the obligatory trips to the Grand Canyon one must make when one lives in Flagstaff and out-of-state visitors come.

I was shooting a panorama with my phone in a vain attempt to capture what cannot be captured when I saw the poor dog.

It was a corgi, low-slung with white fur and larges patches of tan, its sharp ears up, dutifully following along after its person, a young willowy woman in a blue parka and a fluffy white hat.

You might think that it was the woman that held my eye, with her lovely round face and curly wisps of blond hair escaping her hat, but I did feel for the poor dog.

Where it wasn't packed down by tourists, the snow was taller than the dog, the January air so cold it couldn't possibly smell anything, and the view, even if it could see over the low limestone wall, would be lost on it anyway.

It was out here freezing its ass off driven by its domesticated dependency on mankind, this woman in particular, and its inherent pack nature.

Seeing the corgi made me miss Rocky, the shepherd/lab mutt I had grown up with who had died two years back. Yes, I was one of those annoying people who wanted to pet every dog they saw, still feeling like a part of me, an important part of me, was missing since he left.

"He must be so cold," I said as I approached, putting my phone away and regloving my freezing hands. She looked at me, a smile playing on her red lips, her ice-blue eyes meeting mine, and suddenly I didn't feel quite as cold.

"Can I pet him?" I asked, pantomiming in case she was one of the many foreigners that pack that Canyon, although the weather had thinned things out mightily, so it wasn't crowded for once.

She smiled and nodded and it took some effort on my part to not stare at those fine, elfin features and pet the dog.

I took my right glove off and pet him. "Poor fella, you must be so cold." His fur was coarse but clean, his deep brown eyes looking right into mine and looking a bit sad, but just like he understood everything I was saying. His dog collar had "Aspen" embroidered on it. "How are you liking the Grand Canyon? Is it everything you hoped? Seeing everything you wanted to see?"

"Well…" a lilting feminine voice answered, "meet me back here at midnight and I'll tell you all about it."

I looked around shocked to hear the woman speak, but it had to be her, there was no one else here. I looked up, her shining blue eyes met mine and I wasn't cold at all. Not one bit. She smiled and nodded in the direction she had been going and I just smiled like an idiot. After a few steps, I heard her say, "It will be a night you never forget." She turned and waved giving me a smile that made my heart thud like I had just run a 10k.

So, she wanted to meet me on the freezing cold rim of the Grand Canyon at midnight when there would be not one thing to see. Who was I to say no?

"Ben!" My mother called from the other direction. "Benny, I want you to meet Mrs. Callahan, she's from Flagstaff." Being called "Benny" sent a chill down my spine, but I indulged myself and watched the elfin woman walk away with her corgi by her side before seeing what my mother wanted.

———

Leaving our canyon view room required a way-more-than-awkward conversation with my mother and father. We were, unfortunately, sharing a room, my folks sprawled on their bed watching the Golden Globes. My father with his bifocals on, mostly reading a thick Thomas Jefferson biography, and my mother giving a running commentary on the women's fashion choices that neither my father nor I had any interest in.

"Where are you going?" she asked, a neutral expression on her face. It was almost ten, two hours before the rendezvous, but there was no way I was going to try to sneak out at 11:45 and answer awkward questions then.

"A date."

Her right eyebrow raised, and she sat up straight against the shelf of fluffy white pillows propping her up. She brushed her shoulder-length blond hair behind her ears. My mom is super fit and wears her fifties very well. My feet were sore from tromping after my folks for miles and miles on the rim that day. "Is this one of those…those 'Tumbler' things? You know, swipe one way of you like them and…you know." She flapped her hands like the rest was too dirty to even speak.

"No, Mom. It's called Tinder and I met her on the rim today." I was twenty-four, way too old to be interrogated about the dating norms of my generation, and not nearly old enough to talk to either of my parents frankly about sex.

And that got my mind turning and hoping this elfin beauty had her own room because coming back here would be impossible.

"You have protection, I trust," she said, more than a hint of amusement in her brown eyes.

"Yes, son," my father piped up, looking up from his book over his glasses. Dad was a bit pudgy around the middle with a splash of grey invading his short black hair, but almost as fit as my mother. They were both determined to do a better job of aging than their parents had. "You must have protection these days."

My cheeks flushed hot and I realized that, no, I did not have any protection. Not only were my parents embarrassing the hell out of me—which I think they actually enjoyed—but they were right. So, I guess I knew what I would be doing for the next two hours—sprinting to every gift shop still open in a vain hope that they had some Trojans behind the counter. And if that failed, approaching twenty-somethings still wandering around to see if I could buy one and not come off as a completely desperate creep.

At least I would have something to do while I waited for midnight to roll around.

———

The Grand Canyon is a presence, even when you cannot see it. The clouds were thick, the night air sharply cold, but the wind had stilled making it bearable. Standing on the rim where I had met the young woman and the corgi, I could feel the canyon even though I couldn't see it. Maybe it was the way sound traveled, maybe it was the slight breeze floating up out of the nothingness, maybe it was the black hole quality where sound and light just seemed to disappear, but whatever it was I could feel the vast void in front of me.

I could see how this could be romantic. One of the seven wonders of the world; an empty nothingness in front of you on a freezing cold winter's evening. The Grand Canyon was still grand even in the dark.

I paced, my not-so-new jacket a little light for extended time outside. My feet still hurt, and I was careful to stay on the hard-packed snow and not hit any ice patches. Best not break an arm before she showed up. There was just enough light coming from the lodges behind me to see.

Midnight came and passed, and the cold was getting to me, the dropping temperature causing the air to sting my nostrils as I breathed. This storm had been unusually prolific and unusually cold.

I stamped back and forth deciding to leave at least ten times when I heard, "Oh you waited. I had some trouble getting out of the room."

I stopped and looked around for my elfin beauty, but she was nowhere to be seen.

"What the…" I mumbled taking a step forward and almost running into something. I looked down and in the dim light I could see the outline of an animal. A dog. A corgi.

"Aspen?" I said, still wondering where his owner was.

"Yes indeed," the voice said. "Who where you expecting?"

My mouth dropped open and I sucked in a breath, the cold air sharp in my lungs, my teeth aching.

"And my name is not Aspen," the voice went on. "It is Angelica Huston."

I spun around again, my foot catching on an ice patch and I almost went down.

"Are…are you talking to me?" I asked the dog.

The dog barked, licked my hand, and then I heard, "Well you're not quite as dumb as you look, Benny. Follow me."

———

Dogs don't talk. They don't arrange meetings on the edge of the Grand Canyon with grad students. They don't speak in the sweet voice of an elfin goddess. And they most certainly don't call me "Benny."

But Aspen was…excuse me, "Angelica Huston" was talking to me. And he was a she. And she trotted along the rim to the east past the El Tovar and the shops until we were in the forest, the trees still covered in the marshmallow-like puffs of snow.

My mother has been obsessed with baking shows lately. The only reason my folks had watched the Golden Globes was that the wifi up there was godawful and my father doesn't know how to turn his cellphone into a hotspot—and I wasn't going to lend a hand, needing a break from all the reality show confectionery competitions.

These are the kinds of things that occupy your mind when you are following a telepathic dog along the dark void that was the Grand Canyon that night.

Besides, what was I going to do? Go back to the room and crawl into bed not giving one more thought as to how a dog can speak to me.

"Almost there," Angelica Huston said.

"Where is there?" I huffed back, having trouble keeping up with the short-legged canine on the snow packed trail.

"You'll see."

"Where is the woman you were with?" I asked.

"Sleeping. She likes to sleep. Useful that one, but not the brightest bulb, if you get my drift."

Is this what dogs think about their owners? "Not the…"

"But you two probably would have done alright. You are pretty enough and shallow enough to be just her cup of tea."

And the corgi definitely has an English accent. Subtle, but definitely nice. My stupid hormone-addled mind wondered if the elfin woman also had a lovely accent to go with those lovely eyes and long legs.

The path started to gain some elevation and I had to focus to keep up with the dog and then something occurred to me.

"Is your name really Angelica Huston?"

The corgi barked out a laugh. I mean it was a real bark, but I swear it sounded like the dog was laughing at me. "You are a real rocket scientist aren't you? No. My name is not 'Angelica Huston.' I just happen to believe she's a fine actress that never got the recognition she deserved. Besides, my real name is something your human vocal cords and monkey pallet couldn't properly handle."

There was a brief pause while I huffed up the hill. We were

about a mile away from the South Rim Village and almost halfway to Yavapai Point. Basically, in the middle of nowhere.

"Angelica Huston? You mean from the old Addams Family movie?"

The corgi stopped and eyed me, a long growl rumbling out. "She was excellent in that movie, of course, but I suggest you sample some of her less commercial work. Say, her Academy Award-winning performance in *Prizzi's Honor*. Now crack on, mate. Almost there. I promise this is something you don't want to miss. Admittedly not quite what your hormone-addled human body was hoping for. I could smell your pheromones over your awful body spray, but I did promise you a night to remember.

Angelica Huston sped up her trot and I scrambled up the hard-packed snow path to keep up with her.

———

Jumping off the rim of the Grand Canyon is too much to ask, even if you are a telepathic corgi with an English accent named Angelica Huston.

I followed the corgi until we got to what I knew was a spectacular overlook, the snow beaten down by the many feet that had been there—including my own earlier in the day—so that some rock on the ledge was visible.

Angelica Huston turned to me, her tongue lolling a bit, her breath coming fast and steaming out in clouds of condensate, some snot leaking out of her black nose, looking like nothing more than a short, tired dog.

And then it occurred to me. The clouds where thick and we were far away from any major light sources and yet I could see fine, the landscape clear if a bit monochromatic.

"Are you helping me see?" I asked.

The dog nodded. "Maybe you aren't as dumb a sod as I

thought. Oh well. Let's do this. I promised you a night you won't forget, Benny. Follow me!"

Angelica Huston ran across the flattened snow and bare rock, her short little legs carrying her as fast as they could, and leapt into the void.

I stood there, justifiably dumbfounded, waiting to hear something in the cold night, like the sound of a twenty-five-pound dog landing on snow covered rock. Or a yelp. A cry. A crash. Anything.

The night was preternaturally quiet, the wind not stirring, only the distant sound of a car braving the snow-covered roads.

No. It wasn't a car, the sound somewhere between a whine and whoosh, slowly building in volume and coming from the dark void where Angelica Huston had leapt to her death.

And then I could feel it. The void didn't feel so empty anymore as the sound became louder.

And then I saw it…a shape rising out of the darkness, glowing silver in my strange monochromatic vision. It was maybe seventy yards long, ten yards wide, the end facing me bulbous and wider. On top of it was said corgi barking its fool head off.

The ship rose—for it was clear at this point that this was some kind of flying vehicle—gracefully in the air.

"We tried this the easy way, my friend," Angelica Huston said, her voice as clear as if she were right beside me. "Hold on!"

The craft was hovering about twenty feet above the rim, a wash of warm air blowing against me, when I felt it. A lightness. At first it was exquisite, like I was suddenly light on my feet and could run forever. And then my stomach turned on me, my gorge rising, making me regret my Mexican food dinner, and I was floating in the air. I was swept off the ledge, the dark void of the canyon below, vertigo upon me making me think I was falling when I was, in fact, rising. When I was under the ship floating up to it, the vertigo mounting and my vision tunneling in, the last thing I remember thinking before I passed out was…"Is that thing shaped like a bone?"

————

My head hurt and my throat burned like it was spring break and I had drunk way too many rum and cokes and had spent the night kneeling at the altar to the porcelain god.

I moved my jaw and felt something crusty on my skin, further reinforcing the spring break scenario.

I woke slowly, the surface underneath me gave a bit, definitely not a bed, but I was glad to not be waking up on the cold tile of a bathroom floor. I smelled…it's hard to describe but it was a warm, earthy smell, a happy smell, something definitely biological in nature. I felt and then heard movement, and something started to lick my face. No, many somethings started to lick my face and consume the remnants of my prayers to the porcelain god.

I felt fur rubbing against my skin and that made me think of corgis and the strange dream I had had about a talking dog that called herself Angelica Huston.

The licking intensified as did the loamy scent. It became extreme, tickling me and forcing my mind all the way back to consciousness. I opened my eyes and was staring at multiple bundles of fur close up as they continued to wash my face as if I was a puppy.

I propped myself up on the springy surface and soon discovered it was the bundles of fur that were the puppies, which explained the lovely smell. They crawled into my lap and leapt up on my jacket continuing their mission of cleaning my face.

There were a dozen of them, round, warm and wriggling. All different colors and breeds. Energetic and bouncy. Happy in the extreme. I couldn't help but smile and then laugh and then my head didn't hurt so bad.

The world seemed like a happy and safe place for the first time in a long time. I felt lighter than I had in ages.

The room had a low ceiling, there was no way I could stand up straight, and there were no square corners, everything round. I smelled some other scents in the air, not puppy smell, but something sharper that my nose could not figure out.

The room was oval shaped and plain. The walls a light grey, the floor and ceiling a darker grey.

Where was I?

A round opening appeared in one of the walls and in trotted Angelica Huston. "Ahh...alrighty then. You are awake. Let's get to this, shall we?"

The dog's mouth didn't move, its voice just materializing in my head, shattering my "it had all been a dream" illusion and waking me up further, memories of dangling weightless below a bone-shaped space ship—really that is what it had to be—while I puked my guts out into the void of the Grand Canyon before passing out.

The puppies had apparently finished cleaning me, their saliva dripping down my chin, and scampered out the round door.

"What...I..." I mumbled. None of this made any sense.

"Come on now then," the corgi said—or telepathed, or whatever the best way to describe it is. "Buck up. We've got a lot to do. Remember I did promise you an unforgettable night."

The corgi trotted out of the room and I had no choice but to follow, the ceiling being so low I had to do it on my hands and knees.

———

"Where am I? Who are you? What is going on? Why were those puppies licking me?"

Crawling on my hands and knees, it was very hard to keep up with Angelica Huston, her four legs, although quite short, giving her a distinct advantage. At one point she stopped in front of a few holes in the grey wall and sniffed giving me a chance to catch up.

She turned, her brown eyes looking a bit sad.

"On an interstellar spacecraft. Like I said, call me Angelica Huston. I am trying to help your pathetic ape species. Because you were a mess and we needed some DNA samples."

I blinked, winding back to my questions and matching them up to the answers. "The puppies were taking DNA samples?"

The dog barked, another one of those laughing barks. "Well…yeah. And delivering some calming agents to your dermis via their saliva. Remember when I licked you on the rim and you could see in near darkness?"

I nodded dumbly because I felt very, very dumb. My DNA had been sampled and I had been drugged via puppy licks. They had chemicals that could enhance human eyesight. What the hell? Had someone slipped a magic mushroom in my now evacuated Mexican food dinner?

A greyhound ran up to us, Angelica Huston and him doing a brief circular dance where they sniffed each other's butts and barked, before the greyhound sprinted off.

"Come on now," she said, heading back down the hallway.

The corgi led me into a room with a ceiling just high enough for me to stand, for which I was grateful, but when I saw a human-sized table and a strange segmented hose with a nozzle on the end hanging from the ceiling my ass clenched tight despite the drugs they had given me.

"What…Oh…No…I really don't think so," I said, backing toward the door.

I'd seen some bad reenactments on YouTube of little green

men with big heads and huge eyes sticking instruments in humans where the sun doesn't shine.

"Come on, Benny," she said in my head, "don't make me lick you into unconsciousness. I want you to remember this unforgettable night. I did promise after all."

I looked around, the long passage we had come through behind me. The ship was not decorated in the least and the only two doors I had seen were between these two rooms. I had nowhere to go.

"But why...?" I mumbled.

"We need a sample of your microbiome. Important stuff, that."

I started feeling a bit drowsy and rubbed at my face where the puppy brigade had licked me, the drugs really kicking in.

"Micro...why...?"

"Microbiome, you know, the colonies of critters that live in your gut, help digest your food, do a lot to make you who you are...stuff your kind is just starting to figure out."

I stood there feeling a touch dizzy and more than a touch high.

"Butt bugs," I said laughing.

Angelica Huston nodded.

"But...why?"

"Take your pants off, Benny, get on the table. I'll tell you all about it."

I did what Angelica Huston the telepathic corgi said. It made no sense but what else was I going to do? I saw the little dog approach a small, low platform at the end of the bed and insert all four paws. The table lowered and the segmented tube sprang to life. Instead of freaking out, I just laughed.

"So all this anal probing has been you guys?" I asked.

"Think about it, genius," the corgi said. "How do dogs greet each other. Ever wondered why? There's a lot to be learned down there."

My mind parsed through all the crazy alien conspiracy stuff I had heard about.

"And that cattle mutilations. Is that you guys too?"

She barked out one of her laughs. "Oh no. That's the felines. They like to play with their food, you know."

Right then the small end of the snaking tube connected with my butt and despite the drugs this wasn't so funny anymore. I gritted my teeth and lay there like a good boy while Angelica Huston did what needed to be done.

———

I can't say how bad it was, the anal probing that is. I don't have a good scale for it. After it was over Angelica Huston said, "You were such a good boy. How about a treat?" A piece of bacon fell out of the ceiling, right into my hand and I gladly ate it.

After I got dressed, I crawled after her through the hallway into a larger room populated by a bunch of dogs. The greyhound I had seen earlier, a pug, a shepherd mix that reminded me of my Rocky, and a springer spaniel. They were all on small raised platforms, their paws stuck in them and raised nozzles that seemed to emit the strange smells I had been detecting, their noses wiggling and working hard.

One of the curved walls showed a grainy black and white view of the earth's surface. I could see the winding cut of the Grand Canyon and to the south the thrust of the San Francisco Peaks.

The view was fascinating to me, but the dogs weren't paying much attention to it.

Angelica Huston exchanged a few barks with the other dogs and then sat down. I sat next to her.

My head had cleared, but I was just plain confused. "So… there are no little green men from outer space. Just dogs and cats."

"Pretty much," Angelica Huston said in my head.

"And then why all the stories about the scary green men?"

Her head bobbed, and I swear she was shrugging her shoulders. "You gonna run home and tell everyone a corgi stuck a probe up your butt? Besides, all you humans have a raging ape bias. Opposable thumbs and all that crap. No surprise everyone says it's these scary green men."

"And why me?"

Again that weird doggy shrug. "Why not you? It's not like it was hard with that human of mine. You apes and your eternal need for coitus. Frankly, I haven't a clue how it doesn't drive you all mad. A regular, but brief heat is much more civilized."

She stared at me with her head cocked and then barked at the dogs and they barked back.

"Yeah. We think that's it. You apes are in heat all the time and that makes you all mad and stupid."

She sat there sniffing in silence, the strange, sharp smells too subtle for my nose to delineate anything useful. I also noticed some high-pitched sounds that were just beyond the edge of my hearing.

Not thinking about it, I started petting Angelica Huston. When I got behind her left ear she leaned in and groaned contentedly.

The grainy view slowly began changing as the Grand Canyon got closer and I could start to make out the South Rim Village nestled into the scalloped edge of the canyon, still snow covered and beautiful.

"You're nice and healthy," she finally said, "but I would suggest that you eat more vegetables."

I sat there staring at her, Angelica Huston sounding way too much like my mother.

"We'll be there soon," she said. "So, any more questions, Benny?"

"Dogs and cats are aliens," I said holding up one finger.

"Dogs are fascinated with the human microbiome." I held up another finger. "Cats like to play with their food." I held a third and then a fourth finger. "And Angelia Huston is a tragically underused talent."

"I think you got it."

"But...I..." I mumbled. "Why are you all here. It's not like you all live that long, why waste your time on us?"

The room got silent and I could feel the stares of all the dogs on me.

Angelica Huston huffed out a sigh, her brown eyes so sad.

"We could live longer, Benny. Some of us do. But you apes are so afraid of dying, we choose a shorter life so you can learn."

I sat there on the spongy floor my jaw open. Rocky's death had changed me, no doubt about that.

"Imagine your lives without us," she went on. "We're content with a pet and a walk and some crummy dog chow. We are excited to see you every time you come home. We remind you to exercise and show you how to relax. How much worse a mess would you all have made of this world without us?"

I nodded, feeling strongly the void that Rocky left in my heart and my life when he died. I was a better person when Rocky was around.

Angelica Huston licked me and I got drowsy and peacefully fell asleep on the bridge of the femur-shaped canine spaceship.

———

The day dawned bright, the storm having cleared, the startling blue of the Arizona winter sky back. I awoke to that view, on my back lying in the snow on the rim of the Grand Canyon in front of the El Tovar lodge, some Japanese tourists pointing at me and whispering.

I lay there for a few breaths, the memories rushing back, my world feeling very different than it had the night before. I wiggled my fingers and my toes. I was very cold, but everything seemed to be in proper working order, although I will admit that my butt was rather sore.

I slowly sat up and waved at the next batch of tourists gawking at me and noticed that there were no tracks leading to my location in the middle of what must be a garden.

Angelica Huston and her canine cohorts had unceremoniously dumped me here from their spaceship. Probably using their anti-gravity ray—or whatever they hell they called it—to get me here.

I got up and brushed myself off and walked out to the rim and stared at the majestic grandness. The snow had retreated quite a bit from the lower levels, but the sun on the moist rock intensified the colors there, while the sugary coating on the upper half sparkled in the sunlight.

"There you are," my mother said, a stylish wool scarf wrapped around her neck. "We were worried."

"Good date, Son?" my father asked with a nod and a barely contained smile.

"Yeah. Fine." My mind wasn't on the willowy elfin blonde, but something a lot shorter and a lot furrier.

"We're just heading for breakfast," Mom said, pointing to the hotel. "Hungry?"

I nodded and we walked toward the century-old wooden building. "So, I was thinking, isn't it about time we get another dog?"

My mother stopped and grabbed my arm, giving me one of those super serious looks. "What? You said never again after Rocky. Your father and I...well we would have, but you..."

"I know, but...well...maybe we get one now. Like soon. The next time I'm in Cali. You guys keep it until I get out of school and land a job."

My father put his arm over my shoulders. "That must have been a hell of date, Ben."

I nodded. "I guess you could say I spent the evening around dog people."

My mother smiled and my father pulled me into one of his side hugs. "Let's get some coffee and talk all about it," he said.

Before we walked in, I turned back and took in one last look at the grandest of canyons and marveled at the miracles all around us.

MAGNITUDE AND INSIGNIFICANCE

ROB VAGLE

I am happy to say that we are lucky to have veteran writer Rob Vagle appear regularly in Pulphouse Fiction Magazine *and in* Fiction River *with his really twisted and often head-shaking stories.*

This wonderful little gem is the second dog/alien story in this volume, but looked at from an entirely different perspective.

———

They got into the house because the dog picked up their space ship as if it was its new toy, and carried it inside.

Earth was a place with much green and vegetation and huge oceans. Their ship was one of many, hordes of them, from a planet light years away from Earth. They settled into the backyards, one ship for every domicile. They found the earthlings huge and frightening. But these aliens, the crowleys, found comfort in their size to lie in wait and observe the people of Earth.

Crowley Sig had landed the ship in a yard on the North American continent, near the Pacific Ocean, in a country they called the United States of America. On his descent, when the land was just going dark with night, his readings told him there were no life signs in the backyard. He landed close to the house in a forest of grass. Between the ship and house stood a wall of green, but he could still see the roof and upper floor looming over the wall.

Crowley Sig had a crew of twenty aboard and enough equipment to establish a small colony. And machinery to generate power. Not that they wanted to settle here. If the humans were hostile they would have to be exterminated. If they could be convinced to work with the crowleys, it would be a benefit considering their size. However, the size of the humans was a danger. The poor shape their planet was in pointed to low intelligence of the dominating species. Not good either.

Sig wanted this place to be a new beginning. As he watched the Earth sky shifting from blue to pink to black over the peaked roof of the human domicile, a feeling of peace came over him. It was almost like he had reached home. After many light years and dozens of failed settlements, he felt this had to be it. Home. He knew it was irrational. He was simply tired of searching.

He let the wash of peace flow over him as he watched the colors wash from the sky. Perhaps he let it last for too long. For the crew members beckoned for additional orders.

Sig was in serenity.

Until the dog picked up the ship.

Dogs were companions to the humans, domesticated, which was something the crowleys knew they were not interested in. Dogs were not only used for companionship, but also did work for the humans. They were smaller than humans (still giants to the crowleys), walked on four legs, and they had sharp teeth.

And Sig's ship with a crew of twenty fit in the dog's mouth perfectly.

Its teeth cracked the ship's fuselage. When the dog shook its jaw, the entire cockpit became a clamor of alarms, lights, and smoke. Sig was thrown to and fro in his seat, only saved by the restraints. His crew members screamed and some bounced off the walls.

Sig smelled rancid air and he thought Earth was no longer beautiful. It smelled like death.

Outside the cockpit windows, the view changed to a well-lit human domicile. The floor was made of wood slats. Furniture loomed like mountains at the edges of the rooms.

Everything outside the windows spun before Sig's eyes.

Then the ship dropped from the dog's jaws. The wood slat floor slammed against the nose of the ship. The ship's communications were filled with warnings about breaches in the hull in several locations. There were casualties and emergency medical personnel were needed. Pings from other ships in other backyards were asking if Sig's ship was secured and entrenched.

"It's too much," Sig said. "This place is death." The peace he had felt seemed like eons ago.

He looked around the cockpit for his copilots and navigators but nobody was moving. Humps of flesh were puddling on the floor. His console announced in flashing red lights: engine explosion imminent.

The ship began evacuation procedures. For anybody still left alive, that is. Sig braced himself to be jettisoned.

Outside the cockpit windows, a human form walked up to the ship, their two feet, while looking soft enclosed inside some fluffy material, pounded like thunder on the wood slats.

A human hand gripped the ship and lifted it in the air. Sig found himself staring into the face of a human male. It looked hideous with its smooth skin and lack of hair. And its eyes looked dark and foreboding.

Sig had one moment to take in the awe of a human face. It was enough to last a lifetime.

For the cockpit shuddered as the top blew off. The human's eyes grew bigger, which Sig didn't think was possible. Then Sig, strapped inside the pilot's chair, was jettisoned into the air.

He didn't know where he would go or if he would be able to survive here. First, he had to get away from the human. Instead of being thrown away from the human, Sig found himself rocketing toward its face.

The human's mouth opened and sent a rush of hot breath that smelled sour. A human's mouth looked like a horrible place, dark and red and glistening with formidable white teeth.

Sig thought for sure he was going inside the mouth, but a sharp intake of air from the human's nose pulled Sig up into the nostrils.

The nostrils were darker than the mouth. And more hairy.

Not to mention the glistening mucous he found himself sailing toward.

Sig in the pilot chair ricocheted off the walls of the left nostril, tearing through the hairs, dragging through the mucous.

The human sneezed and the rush of air sent him back out of the nostril and he plummeted to the floor.

He lost consciousness before impact.

When Sig regained consciousness he didn't know how long he had been out. But he did know the sky was light again with an intense blue that hurt his eyes. He was on his side still strapped into the pilot seat and beneath him the ground trembled. The ground was soft and he was tangled up in fur. When he turned his head he saw the dog's tail wagging high above him.

An alarm pinged from the armrest of his seat. When he looked down at it he could see there was a search party looking for him. Probably a crew from another ship in another backyard, probably next door. All Sig had to do was press a button to send a signal. He pressed the button. The alarm still pinged. He pressed it again. Nothing changed. The search party wasn't getting his location reading. Frantically, he pressed the button again and again with no indication of his location being received.

Sig was tired and he had aches emanating from a thousand different places on his body. He had to do something before he lost consciousness again. They had been searching for him the long Earth night and they wouldn't search forever.

Sig tried radio transmission but they couldn't hear his voice. He managed to receive their radio transmissions and the message was bleak: after a loss of two hundred and twenty-six ships and five hundred seventy-four crowleys crushed under human feet, the Mother Commander called for abandoning Earth.

Sig needed no convincing. He had already determined this place was death.

However, since he couldn't make contact with the rest of the fleet, he had to make himself seen by the rescue ship.

He had one final option. The flare gun inside a side compartment of the pilot chair provided for this very purpose when technology failed.

Sig was jostled on the back end of the dog as it ran through the human's yard. Sig looked ahead, beyond the dog's flopping ears, and saw what the dog was chasing. It was the rescue ship, round and green, and flying in a searching pattern no more than two feet above ground.

Sig pulled out the flare gun and shot forward, over the dogs head, between the two flopping ears. With a bang, colors exploded overhead.

The dog howled and crumpled to the lawn where it rolled, and Sig was tossed into the grass. He sank deep in between the blades of grass where it was dark and cool. The dog bolted in the opposite direction. And Sig frantically searched for another flare.

There wasn't another flare in the side compartment and Sig was ready to curse at the sky. When he looked up, he saw that rescue ship hovering above him.

They saw him. The sequence of blinking lights on the underside of the ship told him so. Using the crowley tractor beam technology, the ship picked Sig up out of the grass. The bay door above him opened up and welcoming crowley faces stared down. Sig smiled.

He would be going home. Wherever that might be, to be determined. But it wouldn't be Earth with its lumbering giants who couldn't identify intelligent beings right before their eyes.

LET THE FAMILIES BE JOINED

JOE CRON

Joe Cron, without even seeming to blink an eye, created one of the wildest and most fun stories in this already crazy volume of alien stories.

That's right, this wildly original story is about the alien named Garley, and his inability to make a penis. Not kidding.

Crappy work, crappy food, constant belittlement, you name it. Garley's life was a miserable wreck. Every. Single. Day.

All because he couldn't make a penis.

He couldn't make anything out of his body, but out of the trillions of things he couldn't make, the only one that truly mattered was the penis. If he could manage a sex organ, he could reproduce, and that would elevate his status like nothing else.

Really, the only reason he was even still alive was that he was a member of the royal family. Shift cripples were not at all common, and most of them were simply executed. It was another mouth to feed, and an embarrassing one at that. Too much of life depended on changing, reproduction most of all.

Garley was a shapeshifter. Well—his species was. His planet was Dafton, and his people were Dafters. Born in a stable humanoid form, at puberty came the ability to morph into virtually anything. Not overnight; it took months, and required practice, but most Dafters were so excited by the onset of the change that practicing didn't require any special motivation. It was at puberty that Garley, and everyone else, discovered he was a shift cripple. The ability to change any part of his body was utterly lacking.

What did change was how everyone treated him.

At the moment, Garley was swallowing a bite of beef jerky, ferried from Earth and personally commandeered from the palace kitchen, while attending his older brother, Shit-for-Brains—wait, no, that was only Garley's name for him—Morford, in the royal bedchambers. Garley had been reluctantly afforded the opportunity to be in the bedchambers that day, but wasn't welcome at the grand dinner, so appropriated beef jerky was it for the time being.

The bedchambers were a time capsule. Opulent, as was everything in the palace, but in a completely different way. Huge, ornately crafted king bed that was carved stem-to-stern from a single mahogany tree, hundreds of years earlier. The crafting was exquisite, not only in the artwork, but the scope, as the single-piece frame included a tall canopy, dressed with billowing drapes of pink silk and accents of delicate white lace.

Area rugs fashioned from the hides of various ferocious animals lay on rich, dark, weathered hardwood floors. The grey, stone walls had tall windows with a combination of clear and brightly colored stained glass, also from hundreds of years earlier. Adorning the walls were many dozens of plaques with the names of all the royal couplings celebrated in that room. The only other furniture was four small, wooden stands in the corners, each holding a very old iron candelabrum of five lavender-scented candles burning serenely and filling the room with a pleasant floral aroma.

Oddly enough, the royal bedchambers were only used a few times in every generation, on royal wedding days. As a boy, Garley was anxious for his chance to see it. After the change—or lack of, as the case may be—he became quite a bit less enamored of it. Eventually, he saw it as a symbol of royal excess; a room no one used that was worth as much as entire villages.

Garley had to lobby heavily for the chance to be there. Not to see the room, impressive as it admittedly was. He appreciated the history evidenced there, but had long since been put off what others saw as the inherent appeal of finery. The important part was seeing Shit-for-...um, Morford and his bride on their wedding night. That was critical.

Morford was thankfully old for getting married. He was seventeen, and Garley was fifteen. Especially for princes, that was old. Marriage often came very shortly after the ability to consummate the marriage was achieved.

That ability wasn't just in producing sperm for an egg. It was in producing a reproductive organ to deliver it. In their young, stable, humanoid form, male Dafters had no penis. They had to be able to shift to form one. That's why shift cripples were so shunned. No shifting, no sex organ. No sex organ, no procreation. Garley was cursed to be childless, and on Dafton if you couldn't have children, you were considered worthless.

Worthless enough to simply euthanize. Or be banished to the Solid Colony, where a few hundred cripples lived out their days. Cripples were emotionally devastating to their families, because they spent their childhoods like everyone else. Loving, vibrant families would be destroyed by the painful, creeping discovery through puberty that their child was a shift cripple. Most had the defective adolescent put down, to set the whole thing behind them and begin to rebuild their position in society. The stigma was that powerful.

Some, though, couldn't stand to completely sever the childhood bonds, and those families sent their embarrassment off to live in the Solid Colony. Everyone knew it existed, but no one would admit it. Occasionally, parents even had the audacity to go visit their child, though that was always kept desperately secret.

Owing to his royal blood, Garley was extremely rare: a cripple allowed to live with healthy shifters. At a price. He ate leftovers, almost exclusively. Dressed in discarded rags. His room was scarcely a step up from a maintenance closet. He was given menial tasks and beaten if he didn't do them quickly or correctly. And his brother, Morford, even if he did have shit for brains, taught and played with him and showed him everything about being a prince, then turned like cream in the summer sun.

Since confirmation of Garley's affliction, Morford never spoke to Garley, not a single word, without some scathing, childish remark about his condition, followed by annoying, cackling laughter.

Constipation. That was Morford's name for Garley.

"You're nothing but a solid sack of shit," Morford had said a couple years earlier, not long after the diagnosis. "You're not even diarrhea. At least diarrhea can flow and change. You're just a smelly, stiff constipation turd. You're constipation." And the name stuck.

Morford was also fond of humiliating Garley with practical jokes that generally resulted in Garley face-planting in a puddle or some such. If there wasn't time to prepare a joke, Morford just shoved him down. If they were indoors, where there were merely floors instead of puddles, Morford randomly punched him when they passed in a corridor. Then shoved him down, anyway. And it was always followed by the annoying, cackling laughter.

They'd been close. They'd been brothers. Now, nobody treated him worse than Shit-for-Brains. And that stung the most.

He did have a handful of friends on the palace staff, but even many of the servants looked down on him. After all, they were employed in the palace, a high privilege for working-class Dafters, some through multiple generations.

The best days were when he was merely ignored. Fortunately, that happened a lot.

The palace was outfitted with many excellent facilities, one of which was a science lab, one of the finest and most advanced in the kingdom. Only university labs rivaled it. He was intrigued by the natural world, and spent huge portions of his time doing research of his own design. The palace Science Master was occupied with energy beams and propulsion systems and the like, largely ambivalent to Garley, his condition, or his presence. As long as Garley didn't get in the way, didn't disturb royal scientific pursuits, and didn't leave the lab a mess, he was welcome to further his own knowledge as he pleased.

What pleased Garley most was intellectual enrichment, so even in the context of his utter ostracization from the culture he was nurtured for, when he stepped into the lab, he was happy. He belonged there. The satisfaction of being somewhere he belonged was incalculable.

Now he was standing in a room where everyone in the kingdom thought he didn't belong, but that was about to change.

The garments every couple wore to the bedchambers were robes with intricately sewn patterns of leaves and flowers, closed only by a simple cord belt that was relaxed when it was time to reveal the reproductive organs. Women's were already complete. It was only the men's that couldn't be formed until puberty.

Garley was there as the witness. Witnessing the consummation of a royal marriage was a practice from long ago, when stories say there was an incident in the bedchambers and consummation never occurred. As a result, years later, when that fact came to light, the entire royal bloodlines were disastrously affected. For Dafters, marriage doesn't occur through oaths or any verbal commitment. The marriage is in the physical joining. So without consummation, that royal marriage never occurred, families weren't combined, and so forth, with social upheaval as a result. It took generations—and widespread violence—to settle.

Ever since, royal marriages were witnessed. Garley had to

plead and argue and plead some more, but it was finally begrudgingly granted by his parents, the King and Queen, that he could serve as the witness for his brother's marriage.

Morford's intended was a lovely girl named Keldra, with raven-black hair and, by all accounts, a keen intellect. She was thirteen—it was her thirteenth birthday, in fact—and that was the age of marriage, so today was the first chance for these two families to connect.

Garley, wearing the ceremonial robe of a witness, stood to the side in relative darkness and watched patiently as the couple got onto the bed, still in their own wedding robes. Morford rose to his knees to release the cord belt, and it began.

"Where is it?" said Keldra.

"Wait a minute," said Morford, a hint of confusion in his voice.

He shifted his hips around a little, first side to side, then front to back.

"I don't see anything," said Keldra.

"Hang on," said Morford, his stress clearly elevating a bit.

"Haven't you done this before?" said Keldra.

"Of course. Don't be stupid," said Morford.

Another few moments of pensive gyrating produced no results.

"What are you, some kind of cripple?" said Keldra.

Boy, that struck a nerve. Garley smiled.

"No!" said Morford. "I am not a fucking cripple!" He thrust a pointed finger at Garley, the first acknowledgement by Morford that he was even in the room. "He's the cripple. He's the one who can't make one."

Garley then took a step forward, into the shimmering light of a stained glass window, and released his robe cord, revealing a substantial appendage. "Looking for this?" said Garley.

"Yes!" said Keldra.

"No!" said Morford. "That can't be. It's not possible."

"Oh, I think this proves otherwise," said Garley.

Morford's voice cracked with terrified shock and dismay. "How can this be happening?"

"Science," said Garley. "Years and years of research. Nobody paid any attention to me in all the time I worked in the lab. And nobody ever bothered to try figuring out why cripples were crippled before. Just toss them aside and move on. Well, I had the lab and the motivation, and I figured it out. I took the time, I ran the experiments, I proved it out, and I beat it. I know the answer."

Keldra was giggling a little, clearly impressed with Garley and entertained by the situation.

"Hormones," Garley continued, "from the pituitary gland. One in particular. Took forever to isolate it. But once I did, easy to get some in my system."

"But what about me?" said Morford, whining incredulously.

"Well, that took longer," said Garley, "but I figured out how to suppress it, too. Then it was a simple matter to get something into your fancy dinner."

"You little shit," said Morford. "You little constipated shit."

Garley ignored him.

"My lady Keldra," he said, "our families were meant to be joined today. Are you still interested?"

"With pleasure, my prince," said Keldra.

"Excellent," said Garley. "Off the bed, Morford. But I grant you the honor of being our witness."

"No," said Morford. "It's my wedding day."

"Not anymore," said Keldra. "Don't even think about defying him."

After a thought moment, Shit-for-Brains slunk off the bed and stood to the side. "One thing," he said sheepishly.

"What's that?" said Garley.

"Is this permanent?"

"Regrettably, no. But it can be reproduced at any time. Remember that."

"I will, Garley," said Morford.

Garley smiled. "Then let the families be joined."

KNOCK KNOCK POWER

JOHANNA ROTHMAN

Professional writer Johanna Rothman sometimes produces some of the most fun original stories I have gotten a chance to read over the decades. And this one is no exception.

A little green alien, an engineer on a spaceship, and knock-knock jokes. What could possibly go wrong?

———

Sally was enjoying her dream. She was snug and warm in her purple and white polka dot sheets and matching comforter. Given the artistic sensibilities of the people who designed the staff quarters—make that none—she was glad to have a break from the boring white walls and the deep navy blue carpet of the floor.

She was watching the algorithms fight it out in her dream. She knew other people liked numbers. She liked symbols. Symbols didn't lie. Symbols didn't line up the wrong way and give bad results like numbers did.

Sally snuggled into the warmth a little more, feeling happy in her dream. She almost caught this algorithm. Just a little more and she would understand how to organize the data and she could fix the drive.

Even in her dreams, she thought the drive wasn't *really* broken. But fusion was tricky, and it was her job to tune the drive. That's why she was chasing algorithms. You just never knew when the Captain would need another 5%. Okay, with this captain, it was more like 50%. As long as Sally could stay in Engineering, she was fine. Give her machines. No people.

She heard the dulcet tones of her alarm, "Time to wake up, Sally."

She said, "Snooze for five, Stella," and rolled over for the last five minutes of sleep.

She'd been working hard for what felt like days on end, trying to find more power for the drive. She'd had trouble getting to sleep last night, and now that she was in that doze state, she didn't really want to get up.

She smelled something like cinnamon. Appreciative of the odor, she wondered if she would add a little cinnamon to her coffee today. Hot, tasty, smooth, yup, maybe that was worth getting out of bed for.

Her alarm sounded again. "Sally," in a stern voice, "It is time to get up now. You told me not to let you sleep past one snooze." The voice continued. It sort of sounded like her mother. Sally grinned. Even Mom had had plenty of trouble getting her up in the morning.

She rolled back over, opened her eyes and inhaled sharply.

There was a being perched on her night table. Almost even with her eyes.

It sneezed. Three times.

It looked like a small green human—two arms, two legs, a bald head in proportion to its body. It even had a goatee! Add khaki-colored shirt with pockets, just like an explorer and khaki cargo pants, brown lace-up boots. Sally thought she was still dreaming.

Every time it sneezed, Sally could smell more cinnamon. Mucus that smelled like cinnamon? Kinda crazy.

She closed her eyes and shook her head. She must still be dreaming. Okay, it was really time to get up. She opened her eyes again. The small green man was still there.

"Who the hell are you?" she asked.

"Knock, knock."

"What are you, four years old?" she asked.

It looked offended. "Knock Knock."

Sally rolled her eyes. It must be a freaking engineer. "Who's there?"

"Noah."

"Noah who?"

"Noah wheyah I can get a ride on a fusion drive?"

Sally closed her eyes. She must be dreaming. No small green man with the name of Noah was in her quarters. Especially not one who told knock-knock jokes. With some kind of an old Earth accent. She must have made him up. She sat up and gathered the covers around her, arms outside the comforter.

She whispered, "Pinch me and I'll know I'm not dreaming."

She felt a pinch on her right arm. "Ow!" She opened her eyes.

"You said to pinch you."

"I wasn't talking to you!"

Sally took a second to calm down. On the one hand, a normal person would call security, especially since this Noah had managed to blink into existence in her quarters. A normal person wouldn't discuss anything with a little green man with a head cold.

Sally had never been a normal person.

She shivered. The temperature was still set for sleep, and she was still in her pj's. This set was a deep purple T-shirt with Pi—the white text numbers making the symbol. Her matching purple boxers had the day of the week on the tush. She didn't care what day they said—she had seven of them in rainbow colors. That's all she cared about.

"Temperature for daytime, Stella."

"Alrighty, mate."

"Stella, why are you responding like that?" Sally asked.

"It's talk-like-a-pirate day, matey." Stella said.

"No, it's not, Stella. Please return to normal conversational mode."

Stella made a noise that sounded like a sniff. Stella was an AI. She didn't sniff.

Sally looked at Noah. "What the hell did you do to my AI?"

"Nothing," he said, and sneezed.

"Nothing?" Sally asked. "I'm not buying that."

"Well," he said, "while you were sleeping, I had a little

conversation with Stella. Not too many people name their personal AIs, you know."

Sally nodded.

"I wanted to make sure she was okay. And, I added just a little personality to her. After all, with a name like Stella, how normal could she be?"

Sally wasn't sure if she should be offended or happy that Noah had learned so much about her.

Sally's stomach grumbled. "Look, I need to get dressed and ready for the day. I need to eat breakfast. Get to the point. Why are you here?"

"I told you. I need a ride on your fusion drive. I got dropped off—I'm sure by mistake, my ship wouldn't just dropped me in the middle of nowhere—and I need a ride to a place I can get another ship. I can take a little power from your fusion drive, beam myself to somewhere reasonable, and I'll be out of your hair."

"You need me to beam you somewhere, right?"

"Isn't that what I said?"

"No. You gave me a whole bunch of BS about the fusion drive before you got to the beaming. I want to make sure I do the right thing."

Sally paused. "Where did you come from, anyway?"

"Out there," Noah said and waved at the porthole.

"Yuh, space, I got that," she said. "How did you get in here?"

"That's a secret," he said. "I didn't walk through the wall." He sniffed. "No one can do that." He paused. "Maybe I'll tell you later."

Sally narrowed her eyes and looked at him. "I'm having a hard time believing you need a beam to anywhere, if you managed to get inside the ship from outside. There's a lot more I don't understand. But, I need breakfast and coffee."

"I'd like some coffee, too," he said. "Let's get to the mess."

Sally rolled her eyes. "I need to get dressed, and I'm not so sure about the mess for you."

"Spoil sport." He sneezed again, that wonderful cinnamon odor permeating the room.

She pointed to the door, and said, "Leave. I need to get dressed."

He smiled and said, "I can't stay here?" He paused. "I have an invisibility cloak. You won't be able to see me."

"But, I'll know you're here," she said, "dirty old man."

"I'm not old!"

"Even worse. Put on your invisibility cloak and meet me in the mess in 20 minutes."

"You're faster than other girls."

Sally rolled her eyes again. "I do not want to know how many other 'girls' you know." She paused. "There's no way I can trust you."

Sally grabbed him, wrapped him up in the comforter and tied the ends.

"Hey, I can't move!" he said in a muffled voice."

"That's the point," she said. "Stella, let's get me clean."

"Aye, aye, matey!"

———

They arrived at Sally's workstation in Engineering after a quick breakfast. Engineering was huge—the entire width of the ship. The nearest workstation to hers was at least ten feet away. Sally put her insulated cup of coffee in the magnetic ring to the right of her workstation.

She zipped open her pocket and took Noah out. She put him on the left.

He sneezed again, the cinnamon smell noticeable in the cold and bland air. By default and tacit agreement, everyone left Engineering as designed so they could see and smell anomalies.

No posters. No blow-up dinosaurs, which Sally regretted. No toys. Every Engineering department needed toys when they were stuck on a problem.

No nothing out of the ordinary. Except for the ever-present coffee.

On Earth, she'd drunk cold caffeine. That was a little more difficult in space, but coffee was necessary on every ship and she took advantage of it.

Noah sneezed again, and a bit of egg came out with the sneeze. She looked at it, grinned and asked, "What, didn't like the hot sauce?"

He shook his head. "Not at all. You always eat with that spiciness?"

"Only for powdered eggs." She glared at him. "Look, we gotta get you gone, gone, gone. I need to find the algorithm fix and you need to leave. How do we get you on a beam to where you need to go?"

"I told you, I need power," he said. "Unless you have a matter transporter?"

"Nope, not one of those, not yet." She paused. "You need power? Where will you put it? How will you exist in space without a space suit?"

He cackled. "Sally, you don't have much faith in anything, do you?"

"I'm an engineer. I don't have faith. I don't need faith. I need algorithms and data."

Noah shook his head. "Sally, you're losing out on a lot in life."

She grinned, one of those grins that made him afraid for the first time today. "The last guy who said that to me got kicked into next week. You want to join him?"

Noah shook his head. "Not on anyone's life."

He explained that his clothing was actually a space suit. What she thought was his head was actually his helmet.

"But when you sneeze, I smell cinnamon. And, I can see your facial expressions. And, I saw you eat a little. And, drink some of my coffee. How can you do that, big guy?"

"Rub it in, why don't you?" Noah asked. "But being small means I don't need much power. I can bend space just a little with the power I have. That's why I need more power. I can bend space to move where I need to. But I'm low on power. My so-called friends played a prank on me and I don't have enough power to get home."

Sally thought for a few seconds. "Alright. I got it. Actually, I was working on the algorithm to get more power out of our engines. How much do you need and how can you get it into your suit?"

They spoke for a few minutes.

"Well, if I can get another few percent for a minute or so, you'll have enough, right?"

"Yup."

Noah sneezed again.

Sally started to type and change things on her screen. She absently said, "Knock knock."

Noah said, "Really? Now?"

"Got anything else to do?" she asked.

He shook his head.

"Okay, knock-knock."

"Who's there?" he asked in a bored, sing-song voice.

"Hatch."

"Hatch who?" he asked.

"Bless you!" she said and cackled.

He sneezed again, the cinnamon smell even stronger. "That really wasn't very funny," he said.

"Well, I thought it was, and I'm the one helping you," she said. She finished typing with a flourish. "Okay! I think we got something now." She frowned. "We have to get you over to the drive. That's going to be tricky." She leaned into the monitor. "I forgot something," as she continued typing.

"Knock-knock," he said.

"Really?" she asked.

"Knock-knock," he repeated.

"Who's there?" she asked in a bored voice.

"Needle."

"Needle who?"

"Needle little help gettin' through," he said.

At that, Sally smiled. "Okay, that one wasn't so bad." She paused. "I think we got it now. I'm putting you in my pocket. While you're in there, put your cloak on and let's amble on near the drive."

Noah did as she told him.

Sally walked over to the drive. The power was a bright coherent light of light blue. It started below her level and extended to the top of Engineering, where the power converter for the drive was. She whispered, "Any juice yet?"

"Juice?" he asked.

"Power."

"Not yet," he said.

She circled the drive. After a half-circle, she asked, "Anything yet?"

"Nope."

After making a full circle around the power beam, she returned to her workstation. She took Noah out of her pocket. "What's wrong?"

"Your drive is using all the power. Nothing extra for me. We need to get extra power."

Sally thought back to her algorithm dream this morning. "I think I have one or two more things to try," she said.

Her fingers flew across the keys. Every so often, she touched the screen and frowned.

Finally, she sat back and said, "I'm stuck. All the ideas I had aren't working. You're stuck here until I figure this out."

Noah sneezed again. The cinnamon odor was even stronger.

"Why is your smell getting stronger?" she asked.

"Because I'm losing power faster than I can manage my support systems."

She looked at him. He seemed less green, paler.

He hung his head. "I guess this is the end of the line," he said.

"You'd give up that easily?" she asked.

"Well, you're out of ideas and I'm not doing well," he said. He sneezed again.

"Do you understand algorithms? Especially about power?" she asked.

"Of course," he said. "I bend space. I understand what I'm doing."

Sally shook her head. She was glad he understood because she sure didn't get it. "Okay, let me walk you through it." She bent down and opened a drawer below her workstation. She picked up a small yellow duck and put it in front of her monitor."

"What does the duck do?" he asked.

"The duck is for me. When I have trouble understanding something, I explain it to the duck. My colleagues know I do this, so I can explain it to you and no one will think twice about me talking to myself."

"Let me get this straight. You talk to the duck?"

"Of course. What do you do when you're stuck?"

"I talk to other people."

Sally snorted. "Maybe that works for you. Doesn't always work for me."

Noah looked at her. "I don't think much of your people right now."

"Doesn't matter. Let me tell you about this algorithm and you and the duck can help me figure it out."

Sally talked to the duck—and to Noah. The duck never spoke back. But, every time Noah had a question, Sally explained her thinking.

Noah found an inconsistency—a small inconsistency, but one nevertheless.

"Yes!" Sally fist-pumped. "That's it!" First, she ran a simulation. That worked. She rotated the image in front of her. "Okay, I think we got it." She initiated the new algorithm.

Noah sighed and sneezed again. "Sure hope you got it now."

Sally looked at him. His previously bright green skin was now almost a light yellow. Uh oh.

"Hop in," she said, opening her pocket. He continued to sit, so she scooped him up and stuck him in her pocket. "Don't bother with the cloak," she said. "Let's get the most exposure for you."

She walked toward the drive. It looked even brighter to her. Instead of light blue, it shone a bright white. They might even need glasses of some sort down here now.

Sally glanced down as she got near the beam. No change in Noah. She walked around the drive, taking her time, looking at the drive.

After one circuit, she looked down at him. He was brighter, but not as bright as this morning. She walked two more circles around the drive.

"Hey, I'm at full power," he said.

Sally whispered, "Knock-knock."

He whispered back, "Who's there?"

"Tank," she said.

"Tank who?"

"You're welcome," she said.

"An excellent adventure, matey!" he said, and laughed. He gave one more sneeze and then vanished.

Sally turned and whispered, "Bye matey, yourself."

ILENE'S BOX

ALEXANDRA BRANDT

Alexandra Brandt is a regular contributor to Fiction River. *Her stories always seem to be filled with truth and a gentleness that is hard to ignore.*

This wonderful and original pet story gives us a very different look at a possible alien, and a very different outcome, one with heart.

———

Ilene tucked herself up onto the hard orange plastic seat in the pet shelter playroom, echoing the prim pose of the magnificent silver-colored creature on the carpeted tower opposite her. The pose was less comfortable than it looked: the curvature of Ilene's chair actually supported—well, nothing—and its unyielding surface started digging into various places.

Belatedly Ilene thought perhaps this wasn't actually a *human* behavior, crouching on a chair with her borrowed skirt all rucked up.

Glancing around quickly, she slid her feet back down onto the laminate flooring and contented herself with leaning forward instead, intent on her new acquaintance. The little room was empty but for the two of them and nearly silent, although faint sounds of barking could be heard through the clear Plexiglas walls. She could visit the dogs next, if she needed to.

"First question," Ilene said, pitching her voice low, just in case the beaming blonde girl who had let her in—Mia?—was nearby. "How do you feel about your captivity?" She was pleased to note that no edge, no tremble was evident in her voice, although her hand stole to the small, heavy box in her coat pocket for reassurance.

The great, unblinking eyes gazed back at her, nearly as green as her own. Ilene had chosen the current human body for its average shape and color (pleasantly curved and medium brown), but could do nothing about the preternaturally green eyes that came along with her no matter what form she...borrowed.

Sebastian—according to the tag on his cage when Ilene had first approached the cat adoption corner—was clearly wary of her presence. She could see his dainty whiskered nose twitching at her scent. She sniffed the air too, but her human senses only registered that a lot of animals had passed through this place. Probably pissed here, too, judging by the cleaning fluid smell clinging to the floor. She wrinkled her nose and eyed the cat sadly. "I wouldn't want to be here either."

Sebastian, deciding she had passed his test, began to purr and knead his carpeted perch. Without thinking about it much, Ilene found herself standing, reaching out to stroke his silvery fur, invited by the rumbling and the half-closed eyes. It was remarkably soothing, the feeling of his head leaning insistently into her hand.

Ilene's gaze sharpened as she began to understand. "Oh! It is not always like this. You clever creature. They think they own you, don't they? You have evolved and adapted to make them serve you, even with these limits to your sentience. I see this is a working relationship, then."

She sighed and straightened. The cat's look was a knowing one. "I am afraid you are not for me, dear boy. But I wish you well. I am certain you will find yourself a willing sla—" The word caught in her throat, and she touched her pocket again and looked toward the door.

Mia, who had indeed been hovering just out of sight, bounced in and took Sebastian in hand. "He's just a big beauty, isn't he?" she gushed. She didn't seem at all concerned that Ilene had been holding a one-sided conversation with said "big beauty." Ilene filed that away for future knowledge.

"He's incredible," she said, and meant it. The concept of "pet," repugnant as it was, clearly had its willing participants who seemed to make it work. She might speak to others of Sebastian's kind before she decided anything for sure, because it never hurt to be thorough, but Ilene had a feeling that what she sought would not lie with felines.

"I will come back after I talk with my...family," she lied.

Mia nodded as she closed the cage door. "You might want to make it quick," she advised with a wink. "He's going to get snatched up any day. Aren't you, sweetheart?"

Ilene smiled unconvincingly and left the girl cooing over His Majesty. Time to see about the dogs.

———

Lupe was a big mop of a creature, gangly and foul of breath. For some reason Ilene found herself instantly at ease with her, despite her size, smell, and intimidating description: "Part Irish wolf-hound," her tag had read. Ilene knew somewhat about wolves, and hounds, and Lupe was as much of either as Sebastian had been a Siberian tiger.

Ilene also knew, within moments of meeting Lupe, that this creature would not suit Ilene's purposes either. "Bless you, poor thing," she had found herself saying as Lupe's entire body wagged, as the mutt slobbered all over Ilene's hand with barely-contained joy. "You love me already and you've only just met me."

It was sweet, and also so very wrong. From her research—confirmed now by a light touch on Lupe's limited mind—Ilene understood that the instinct of these canines tended toward companionship and follow-the-leader. She understood how humans could respond to this eager full-body adoration with love and protectiveness. And the knowledge was a leaden pit in her currently-human stomach. A ragged hole in her very non-human psyche.

Her fingers gripped the box in its shabby coat-pocket

protection. She knew she was wound so tightly that something was going to break soon. She would blow her cover, or worse. But she had no one to talk to. Not yet.

A sign by the kennels read: "Ask About Walking Our Dogs!"

It was an indulgence, and she hadn't much time. But Ilene couldn't help herself. Shortly thereafter, Lupe was eagerly pulling on her lead, with Ilene resigning herself to touching the cursed leash for practical reasons, as they followed the directions of the overly-helpful (and unusually trusting) pet-shelter employee to the dog park a convenient block away.

When they reached the long slope of sweet-smelling grass together, Ilene and Lupe broke into a run. The wind on Ilene's face reminded her of days long past, when she had still been Ir Hollu Irah, and had chased the wind at Eebri for days on end. But now... Ilene marveled at the feeling of her own legs stretching long and strong, pounding the earth. She had thought Earth bodies to be clumsy. But maybe, just like Lupe galloping beside her with unexpected grace, humans were made for this, too. Ilene picked up speed. She tasted dust in her mouth, heard nothing but a rushing in her ears, felt nothing but the ground jolting her human bones with each step.

All too soon they reached the end of the green. Ilene bent over, working to catch her breath. Lupe, also panting, flopped across Ilene's feet. Ilene's feet responded in turn by informing her that her borrowed shoes had not been intended for activities like sprinting. She eased the dog aside to remove the confining things, wincing, and found a spot on the grass free of stinking piles. It was not particularly isolated, but the nearest humans and dogs were wrapped up in their own play.

"I want to tell you a story, Lupe," Ilene said, once she had regained normal breathing. "Your human...owners would not understand or believe it. But I know you will listen."

She patted the ground next to her, and Ilene's new best friend was eager to oblige. Poor creature, who didn't know any better than to love the ones who stole her agency at every turn.

"There is a planet, far beyond this system of Sol, where the concept of ownership doesn't exist. Every creature on Irah carries weight. Every mind is...fully-realized. Aware." Ilene fumbled with the limits of this human—which one was it again?—English language. But her borrowed mouth couldn't speak the language of Irah, so this would have to do. "There is certainly no such thing as a pet. There is nothing like...slavery." The word was ugly, made uglier by the knowledge that it belonged in this Earthen language. That it had likely been there, in one form or another, since the beginning.

"One creature of Irah—I suppose we would call it a...young female if we sought a human equivalent—grew up in a particularly sheltered corner of this planet, with little contact with the other worlds that could be found through the..."— she ground her teeth. No good words, here, just ungainly ones like "wormholes"— "the doors into space."

Lupe quietly drooled on Ilene's skirts.

Ilene's lips twitched. Ah, yes. Translating *Irahl* thoughts into *human* words for a creature that couldn't comprehend any of them? This made perfect sense.

And yet, this was how the borrowing worked. And Ilene wanted—*needed*—to tell this aloud.

"The young creature's name was Ir Hollu Irah. Its—her body didn't work like this one. It could catch the wind and ride, with a freedom you can't even imagine. The brain could hold... oh, so much more mind than this one." She tapped her head, with its not-unpleasant cloud of dark curls, and remembered what she had lost when she'd borrowed—and become—Ilene. But that memory was vague. One's psyche was only as great, as strong, as broad as the mechanism that could hold it.

And when she returned it to her ship, to her waiting true body, she might never get those lost parts back.

Would it be worth it?

Ilene plucked at a loose thread on her coat pocket, resisting the urge to check and make sure the box remained inside. It was foolish—she could feel the weight of it against her leg. But everything relied on this. It had to be worth all the losses she had sustained so far, mind and soul. It had to be worth it.

Lupe shifted beside her, rolled her deep brown eyes up to her new best friend, nudged Ilene's hand. Ilene left her pocket alone to scratch Lupe's ears, trying to organize her thoughts, knowing Lupe wouldn't care. And yet...

"For all the great capacity of Ir Hollu's mind, she was not... wise. She had such a thirst for knowledge and chafed at her current life. A traveler named Ae came to her part of the world. A well-respected teacher. He was of her kind, but had lived for years on a sister planet through the doors. He filled her mind with stories of worlds upon worlds, some waiting to be visited, some only meant to be studied from afar.

"At any rate, this scholar-traveler Ae represented everything Ir Hollu had never even known to desire. He fed her hungry, curious mind, he swept her away with his attention. She left Irah behind and followed Ae to his home through the doors. She was still so young, and he promised he would educate her. She thought she would spend the rest of her days by his side, a fellow scholar, a partner.

"She also loved him, and that was what destroyed her."

Ilene's back was beginning to ache from her position; this body didn't seem terribly good at much. She lay down on the grass with a long sigh, comforted by Lupe's bulk—and oddly, her very doggy smell. Ilene *could* stop here. Just leave the story, return Lupe to the shelter, and find another creature to interview. Finish what she came here to do. Be completely free at last.

And yet, she kept talking. If there was a chance *he* could hear and know what she now understood… "Humans would recognize what the relationship truly was between Ae and Ir Hollu. They have many words to attach to it: controlling, co-dependent, abusive. But for a long time, Ir Hollu didn't know those words, or any equivalents in her own tongue. And that was the point—Ae convinced her that she was so uneducated, so naive, so *stupid*, that he would have to start her education over from the beginning. This was enlightenment. This was what she wanted, wasn't it?

"So he stripped away all of her autonomy and locked her in his home until she 'earned' her education. This was normal, this was how things were done, he said. He strung her along, handing out approval in tiny doses to keep her striving to please him in all things. It didn't feel right, but she couldn't articulate why it was wrong. And she always felt so stupid around him. She had no choice but to believe everything he said, every example he showed her of how other worlds worked." Worlds like *this* one.

"But he had made an error." Oh, he needed to be listening to this. "He had selected Ir Hollu for her naïveté, her sheltered upbringing, her eagerness to please. But her *curiosity* was the thing that turned the tide. Ae had a great storehouse of knowl-edge, not unlike the human library or even this…Internet. Of course he never let her access it, only dished out knowledge in pieces. But she paid attention to everything, partly out of self-preservation, but also just because of her nature. And one day she figured out how he got into this storehouse.

"By that time, he had started leaving the house for longer stretches of time, no doubt thinking her properly enslaved. And it was true that she had no rebellion on her mind—yet. She was just so hungry, so desperate for *reasons*, that she stole to his repository while he was gone. And then everything changed." She closed her eyes, remembering how she had felt, that punch in her gut when the truth had been blown wide open before her.

"Ir Hollu learned she hadn't been his only so-called 'student.' No, poor innocents stretched back in time, all serving Ae's will, trapped in the emotional cages he created for them. More than once, one had broken and died of misery. Sometimes he discarded them when they were no longer useful.

"At that moment, Ir Hollu knew this cycle had to end. She started to rebel quietly, stealing information piece by piece. Ir Hollu discovered clues at first by accident, and then kept digging. It was a long and harrowing journey, finding the truth. And the truth kept getting stranger and more terrible.

"Ae wasn't even of Ir Hollu's kind at all. He had possession of a kind of technology that can fling a person's consciousness —or mind, or soul—into another living being, essentially borrowing that creature's functions—and some of their identity and personality—for a time."

Ilene smiled, and it felt good. She still couldn't believe she had done this. That she had gotten this far. She had broken free of Ae's cage, and done the unthinkable. The weight of the box in her pocket, the weight in her soul, they were nothing. Nothing. Tears started in her eyes. She curled herself against Lupe's shaggy body and let them fall.

But before she could dry her eyes and resume her story, a voice came from somewhere near her feet.

"Ma'am? You're fifteen minutes overdue to return Lupe." It was the shelter employee, the trusting young man—Chad—who had let her take Lupe out. Ilene quickly sat up. The boy looked annoyed, but quickly softened when he saw the tears staining her cheeks. "I—that is—sorry, ma'am. It's just—"

"Of course. I'm sorry." Ilene hunted for her shoes while Lupe rose to greet Chad with her usual enthusiasm. Ilene let him lead the dog away, a lump in her throat. Ilene had no desire to *own* Lupe. Certainly no desire to use her for the final part of the plan. Still…maybe when it was all over…

No, this was how it had to be.

At the shelter, Ilene apologized again and admitted she didn't have enough money to adopt Lupe after all. She felt raw, incomplete. Telling her story had lifted something inside her, but ultimately fixed nothing. She hadn't finished it, either.

But time was running out. Time to investigate other options, find the match she needed, complete her work, and be free. She only had a day left.

———

She found a pet supply store—no dogs and cats here, just small creatures—and started at one end, methodically making her way to the other. Spiders, snakes, lizards, fish—none of them would do. They scarcely had minds at all, compared to what Ilene—or rather, Ir Hollu—was used to. The cat and the dog hadn't had much brain capacity, either, but in some ways that was preferred. Not too much, not too little. But mostly Ilene needed to find the right…*feeling*…in the right mind.

No time, no time. She kept up the chorus in the back of her mind, moving to the small furry things in the middle of the store. Mice, gerbils, rabbits, guinea pigs. Tiny cages, tiny minds, anxious little creatures dodging the grasping hands of small human children, hiding in plastic shelters or holes burrowed through the soft wood shavings that lined their cages. Their fear spoke to Ilene's gut.

They would do.

She looked around for a store employee. The black-and-white male guinea pig, she thought. She would buy him and be done.

But then she heard a heart-rending shriek from the side of

the store she had not visited yet, and she dropped those plans and followed her ears to a large cage on a pedestal. Inside paced a bird, with stunning red-orange-gold plumage edged in green. The sunset-colored captive paused its movement and looked at Ilene sidelong. They were nearly eye-level with each other, Ilene and the bird.

And she knew.

"Oh, wow." A voice at Ilene's elbow startled her, and she looked down to see a small dark-haired human boy gaping at the bird perched above him. He turned. "Mom! Mom, you *have* to come see this one!"

His mother hurried over, and Ilene moved aside, her heart falling. She should say something—

"I don't think we want a bird, buddy. Sun conures can be really noisy. And what if Edgar caught him and ate him?"

"Awww." The boy looked down, scuffing his shoe on the floor. Then he perked up. "Can I just have him on my shoulder for a minute? Like a pirate? Just for a minute!"

His pleading voice and quivering lip appeared to work on the mother, for a store employee was quickly summoned and the request explained.

"Not a problem," the helper said. His tag read "Josh." "Sunny's wings are clipped so he can't fly too far away, but you'll still want to be careful not to make startling movements. Here, let me get him out for you."

His wings are clipped.

The thought rang in Ilene's mind as Josh opened the cage and carefully coaxed Sunny out. It echoed while they helped the bird clamber onto the boy's shoulder. It whispered while Sunny resumed his pacing, moving from one shoulder to the other while the boy giggled.

Ilene stared at the bird. Even when Sunny left the cage he would be forever trapped. Never able to reach his full potential. The skies would always call to him and he could never—

The boy squealed as a flash of orange-gold feathers heralded Sunny's lunge for... Ilene. Frantic flapping nearly got him the full distance to her arm, but he began to falter. Quickly she reached out to catch him, getting a scratch or two from his grasping talons before he settled. He looked at her sidelong again. Her heart hammered.

"Ow! What'd he do that for?" The boy held the side of his neck and glared at the bird while the store helper apologized profusely.

"Sometimes birds like that prefer certain people, buddy. He seems to like that lady."

Ilene bit her lip. "Can I buy him?" she asked, eyes still on the unhappy beast clinging to her knuckles.

"He's all yours," the mother said firmly, and led her pouting son away.

Josh looked at Ilene quizzically. Maybe there was something off in her tone of voice. "I guess he does like you," he said.

Sunny stayed on Ilene's shoulder while Josh rang her up. The expense made her wince, thinking of her borrowed bank account, but she'd fix that before this was over.

The bird resisted going back into the cage when it was time to go outside. Josh tried to toss him in and close the door, but the resultant flurry of flapping and thrashing ended in Josh nursing a bleeding finger and Sunny clinging to the outside of the cage. Finally they coaxed the bird inside with a treat and quickly shut the door before he noticed.

Ilene felt ill.

It was time—the box would cease to function soon. Ilene drove to her borrowed house. She locked the door and took the cage into the corner bedroom. It was a nice room, tidy and simply decorated in blue and white. One window looked out into a fair-sized lawn with a tall fence, and the other out onto a quiet street. It would be a good place to have a dog.

Ilene shook her head and focused on Sunny. She took the

box out of her pocket and hesitated. Words came out of her, pulled there by a need she couldn't suppress.

"So. While Ae was away, Ir Hollu would steal into his files. She began to research everything that Ae had ever told her was true. She discovered his lies, and also the truths within them."

Of course Sunny hadn't heard the first part of the story. That didn't matter, in the end. The bird wouldn't understand it anyway.

Ilene gripped the box harder. Oh, she wanted *him* to hear this. "But Ir Hollu was even smarter than that. She learned more about Ae's consciousness trick, the technology behind it, than Ae had ever known. She figured out how to—to pull him out, against his will. And one day when he came back, she turned the tables on him."

Ilene tapped the side of the box. Lights winked along the edge, accompanied by a low hum.

"Then she stole his ship, stole his power, and came to Earth, a place that believed in ownership, just like Ae did. A place full of both good and evil, but in the end, a place nothing like Irah." Ilene's voice broke. This was almost over.

"On Earth, she found Ilene, borrowed her for a weekend… and then, she found you, Sunny. Broken little creature that you are. And for that, I am sorry."

This was wrong, so wrong. And yet Ilene's borrowed heart pounded in wild anticipation. All the times she had felt so trapped, surrounded by walls of fear and helplessness, longing for flight, for freedom even while believing Ae when he said she didn't deserve it—all the other beings who had loved him and found themselves betrayed, broken, enslaved…they would all be vindicated at last.

Yes, the tables had turned, now.

Ilene took a long, shuddering breath and pressed the other side of the box. The flashing increased in frequency, lights twirling on each side. The box opened, and she braced herself.

He came screaming at her mind, striking against it with white-hot rage. He wanted to wrestle borrowed Ilene away for himself, to send Ir Hollu hurtling away, to punish her for daring to defy him. But she held firm against his attack and held the box, using its power to keep Ae from leaving the room to find another human to borrow. Forcing him in only one direction.

It was a gamble, thinking Sunny's tiny unhappy mind would be cage enough to keep Ae trapped.

But the psyche was only as good as the mechanism that could hold it.

The bird screeched, eyes sparking a preternatural green. He thrashed, flailed on his perch, and then grew still. Tentatively, fearfully, Ilene touched the edge of the bird's mind.

It was Ae, and yet not Ae. Something of him still remained in that simple brain, but had no capacity for the self-aware consciousness, the soul that had once been. The mind was trapped, and it knew it. Rage and pain dominated what remained behind.

It was horrifying.

It was what he deserved.

Ilene took the cage and its contents back to the pet store, explained that her boyfriend wouldn't let her keep it. The bird inside wouldn't shut up, flapping against the door as if trying to get back to his beloved new mistress.

Soon she would return to the ship, become Ir Hollu again, and let the true Ilene reclaim her body. No harm done.

But first, before Josh took the cage back to its pedestal, she asked if she could have a moment "to say goodbye." The store clerk looked like he wanted to say something, but in the end only nodded and moved away.

For a long time, she stared at her one-time partner, her oppressor, her conquered enemy. Then she leaned in close, forcing him to meet her gaze with a beady green eye of his own.

She smiled.

"Eat your heart out, beloved," she whispered, then straightened and turned. The bird shrieked, fluttered, clawed at the cage. But his wings were clipped. He could not follow.

THE GODDESS PARTICLE

DÆMON CROWE

Daemon Crowe is a regular contributor to Fiction River, *as well as many other major magazines.*

In this second cat story in the volume, Daemon uses the cat/alien relationship in a very strange and disturbing way. Not a bad way, just disturbing.

————

Ba'set shoots out of the transport node and into the designated furry, fat and female host. It takes no time at all, literally no time, since subatomic beings live in the quantum world of twinned entanglement. It nullifies both space and time.

The powers that be assigned a familiar place among the few locations available to her. Her unfortunate excursions to the desiccated fourth and shattered fifth planets in the orbital system of this same yellow star disqualify her for much else. A punishment of sorts, sending her back to the place where the few survivors of her poor performance amongst the macros took refuge.

It is a wonder they let her go at all.

Not this time will she ride the planet's dominant species. She begged for a placement inside their most bonded companion, until fresh data indicated a subservience so thorough it would hamper her independence. She settled, once again, for a species both loved and reviled, both tamed and savage, both typically lazy and weirdly energetic.

She will make the most of this final opportunity to redeem herself.

————

Ba'set—solo energy particle floating far from her entangled twin—wedges herself amongst the native subatomics that comprise her host. Not one entangled pair acknowledges her existence, nor does the macro host recognize the delicate inter-weaving of their beings. She will have free rein over the beast, provided she can keep it awake more than a third of the time.

Why did she disregard what a bore space time and its crea-tures can be? Why did she consign to oblivion how limited their senses, how awkward their bodies, how macro short and insignificant their lives?

Now here, in the macro's reality of space time, she can no longer ignore their illusion of reality, what they have made of it or what has become of them.

Yet, this pseudo reality has its benefits: the warmth of a distant sun on slumbering flesh; the soothing hum of contented creatures; the smell of fish.

She pries open one host visual receptor, twitches its whiskers and sniffs.

The face of a dominant species—male, if the hairy black stubble on the lower part of its face is any indication—leans over her host's head, her head, close enough to feel the mois-ture of the air leaving its mouth, to smell the rank remains of its last meal. She forgot how they reek when first they wake from sleep.

"Morning sleepyhead."

The deep tones from its mouth mean nothing. Ba'set will have to add comprehension of yet another set of the oral noise these creatures use to communicate. This small sample sounds nothing like the language of the pyramid builders or the male that caused her demotion from interactive monitor to hidden bystander.

This male passes a shallow metal cylinder close across her nose. She remembers that odor, although now a distinct metallic tinge contaminates the ambrosia of oily fish.

She opens her jaws in a cavernous yawn and stretches one foreleg in the direction of the metal cylinder.

The male makes a low gurgling sound in the back of its

throat. The corners of its mouth quirk up and both eyes twinkle.

Smile—Happiness? Teasing?

It snatches the fish out of reach.

Teasing.

"Not so fast, Goddess, you old lazybones."

The male retreats backwards on its hind legs toward an opening.

"If you're not still off your feed, come and get it."

The male disappears beyond the opening.

Ba'set opens her second eye. She opens her mouth to capture the lingering fragrance of fish.

Things have changed since her last trip to the third planet of this star. Macro time and travel took her to woven grass huts and mud brick hovels, to one-room wood shanties and intricately laid stone palaces. This small room resembles none of them.

The male has disappeared through the only large opening in four smooth, blank white walls. A smaller opening punctures the wall opposite. Dust motes float in rays of pink light streaming through a blanket of slats covering the smaller opening. The light falls in ribbons across the soft, warm platform she lies curled upon.

She jumps off the soft platform and up onto a hard wooden surface in front of the slatted blanket. Her nose pushes easily through a space between the slats.

A clear, hard liquid covers the opening behind the blanket. Vague memories of window glass zip through her consciousness. Nothing new there.

On the other side, in the world behind her present four walls, she expects birds chirping in a forest of trees, herds browsing in a plain of grass, dominant species toiling in a cultivated field, mountains soaring into a clear blue sky, boats dancing on the bright waters of a flowing river, or maybe the face of another dwelling staring back.

What she sees sends chills down her spine.

A few spindly trees, but no forest. A strip of browned and brittle grass cut too short to survive. On the grass, a dominant's bonded companion chases its tail. Metal chariots belch black smoke as they traverse a dry black river. Across the river, small, buildings of wood squat in near-dead strips of grass. Idle metal chariots sit in rivulets close by their doors.

Too familiar. Too much like the last times of the fifth planet, before the powers that be ordered its destruction. They allowed her to take what she could to the fourth planet before the explosion. Millions of remnants orbit there still.

She shivers as the star rises huge and red, its glow cutting through an atmosphere filled with unnatural particulate. How much like the fourth planet, before water retreated underground or froze on the surface as the atmosphere leached away.

And now number three.

Is she already too late?

She jumps from the wood platform to a floor covered in a soft green finish. Her paws sink pleasurably into it. She saunters through the opening, tail held high, head and ears erect, eyes wide open. She follows the faint smell of fish through more white-walled, soft-floored cubicles filled with what she now calls to recollection as tables and chairs, until her paw touches a cold, hard surface she recognizes as tile in a room like no other she has seen.

The male stands in the middle of the room sipping from a cup and watching images flicker across a flat rectangle mounted on one wall.

"Hungry, Goddess?"

The male never turns its eyes from the images. She guesses Goddess is the name of her host. As good a name as any. Goddess she is.

A disembodied female voice spouts more words Goddess does not understand. She understands the images. Feels their impact.

The heat of fires ravaging vast swathes of forest, burning to the ground dwellings like those across the black river. The taste of sea water as a giant wave breaks ashore and destroys still more. The sting of smoke from a million belching chariots stalled in a vast herd of chariots along a black river. The frenzy of a shouting, heaving throng of dominants pushing against a phalanx of black clad dominants armed with clubs and shields. The stench of burning chariots piled high on a river. The grit of dust as the earth rumbles, buildings shake and collapse.

She tries to blink the images away, but each time she opens her eyes another scene worse than the last appears.

"Here ya go."

The male places a pottery bowl of shredded fish flesh onto the tile in front of Goddess. Her host's stomach grumbles and her mouth waters. The call of the needs of the flesh overpower Ba'set. She gives in to the Goddess.

True to her Goddess nature, she leaves half the fish. With a flick of the tongue and a lick of her chops, she looks back up at the rectangle on the wall. To her astonishment, she recognizes the flickering image.

Rome. The Vatican. A man in white robes waves from a balcony. She knows those gestures, knows they called for peace and goodwill, despite what the other images show.

A warm glow fills her belly.

She wasn't wrong to play the martyr, to die and rise again, not if the message lasted for macro millennia.

But the white figure fades and the images of disaster return.

Her heart sinks to the very depths of her bowel.

Ancient Goddess this host might have been when the pyramids were new. Son of God she might have been when she could still interact with these creatures, who owe their very existence to her intervention when the powers that be destroyed the riot of megafauna, but spared the planet itself. She, herself, once cleansed the planet, washing away all but a chosen few. She swore never again. But...

Flashes and bangs draw her attention back to the wall. A dominant clad in black races along a black river pointing a fire stick at every dominant it meets. They fall writhing or drop in a motionless heap.

Fur rises along her spine. Her tail brushes out.

Enough!

In anguish she reaches across time and space to her entangled twins.

Countless particles heed her call.

———

She has learned from past mistakes. This will be swift, clean, surgical.

At her signal, each particle inserts itself in a virus so deadly not one dominant will survive.

In less than the time it takes the planet to revolve twice on its axis, every dominant and all its closest genetic relatives have sucked down their last breath. Their swollen carcasses litter the landscape. Carrion feeders—vultures, hyneas, Tasmanian devils, Komodo dragons and rats, billions of rats—feast on the remains.

Goddess gives herself a final reward for a job well done. She snares a fat, juicy rodent, savors its warm blood, the crunch of its bones, the sweet tang of raw flesh.

She leaves her host to her gustatory pleasures.

Sometime, when the planet has healed and the once dominant's follies no longer scar its air, seas and land, she will return.

TWO-MINUTE DRILL

DAVID H. HENDRICKSON

David H. Hendrickson is not only a regular contributor to Fiction River *and the major mystery magazines, but a story of his last year was included in the* Best Mystery Stories of the Year *and won the Derringer Award.*

This original and flat crazy story takes on football and aliens, in a way only David could do. I did say that… football and aliens.

———

December 15, 1980
Dallas, Texas

So we was watching that old blowhard Howard Cosell and Dandy Don Meredith on Monday Night Football. There was that other guy in the broadcast booth, Frank Gifford, but we didn't much pay him no mind even though he did the play-by-play. The windbag and Dandy Don was the show and everyone knew it.

We was watching in my doublewide, sitting on my sagging, food- and beer-stained couch, a broken spring goosing Fat Freddie or Jimmy Lee every five minutes so them cranky sumbitches had something to complain about besides the damned Cowboys, who was getting goosed pretty good themselves by the Los Angeles Rams, 21-0. I was about the only one not getting no goosing on account of me sitting on the sofa's good end that was right snug up against the wall with the Velvet Elvis. Hey, it's my doublewide and my sofa, even if it's all an ugly piece of shit with no elbow room. It was also my Lone Star Beer them freeloaders was drinking, empty cans littering the gray carpet that once was new but now has so many dark stains they look like drunken polka dots.

Three empty pizza boxes sat sloppily stacked beside Fat Freddie's end of the sofa. We'd emptied them suckers out by the end of the first quarter, but I could still smell the pepperoni and taste the peppers and onions. While the Rams huddled, we all puffed on our Marlboros, adding to the thick blue cloud of cigarette smoke hanging in the air. Fat Freddie added something extra, lifting one prodigious cheek and letting rip. So much for smelling the pepperoni.

On the TV that was not even a first down away from where we sat, Vince Ferragamo completed another pass. The Rams was kicking the Cowboys all over the damned field.

Jimmy Lee rubbed his close-cropped scalp, then scratched his scraggly beard. "If this don't get no better, I'm callin' it a night after halftime," he said. "After Cosell." Howard Cosell narrated highlights of Sunday's games and none of us ever missed it, not even to empty bladders that felt close to exploding. Even if the sumbitch was a pompous windbag, you had to love the way he said on touchdowns, "He...could...go...all...the...way." I swear, when I had Bobby Sue in the back seat of my crew cab pickup a couple weekends ago, I was hearing Howard saying those same words about me. Course, I never did get in the end zone.

Jewerl Thomas, a rookie for the Rams who was making our linebackers look like girly-men, ran off tackle for six yards.

"Jimmy Lee," I said. "You can leave if you want, but I don't turn this set off until Dandy Don sings 'The party's over.' House rule. Hell, it's the one time that Howard shuts up."

"What are you talking 'bout, Clete?" Jimmy Lee said. "Howard don't shut up even then."

Jimmy Lee might have had me on that one.

"Can't believe I had to hear about John Lennon last week from that gasbag," Fat Freddie said, his jowls jiggling as he shook his head. The color in his cheeks drained, and his lips turned unnaturally pale.

Silence, broken only by Frank Gifford's play-by-play, hung in the air as somber as the cloud of cigarette smoke was thick. We'd all been fourteen or fifteen when the Beatles broke up about ten or so years ago. We'd argued about who was the best one.

I swore it was Paul. Fat Freddie said John. Jimmy Lee, as dumb as the days are long, liked Ringo. We couldn't believe it back then, but Jimmy Lee had said, "If I'm lying, I'm dying," which for us was a blood oath. We was devastated when the Beatles broke up even though we mostly listened to country music. Merle, Willie, and Waylon. The Beatles did have a little Commie in them, but they was still the Beatles. It was almost like breaking up with a girlfriend you really liked. One that let you get to second base.

But that was nothing compared to Cosell's announcement of Lennon's shooting and death near the end of last week's game. The windbag, finally given something to sound pompous about, broke the news while New England lined up for a field goal. The three of us sat there and just stared at each other, unable to say a damned thing.

"Howard ain't never gonna announce something that awful ever again," Jimmy Lee said and we all nodded. Wasn't often that Jimmy Lee said something smart, but he'd done it this time.

As if on cue, Cosell spoke up after another Rams first down.

"Ladies and gentlemen," he said in his trademark nasal voice. "We've been informed by ABC News of a stunning and singular event, some might even say preternatural. Science fiction come to life. An event which illustrates with painful clarity what a trivial, dare I say meaningless, endeavor football and yes, all of sports, truly are.

"Alien spacecraft larger than the very stadium where we are observing this game—and let me repeat, this is only a game— have arrived from somewhere in our vast universe, seeming to appear out of thin air, perhaps even another dimension in the Einsteinian sense."

I glanced at the freshly opened beer in my hand and

squinted at the TV set. I set the Lone Star between my legs. I'd always been able to handle my liquor, but had I just heard what I thought I'd heard? I wiggled an index finger in one ear, then shook my head like a soaked dog spraying water everywhere. I thought I might have heard my brains rattling.

But Howard kept on. "These spaceships are now hovering over major cities across the globe. New York, Washington, D.C., Chicago, here in Los Angeles, London, Paris, Berlin, and reportedly Moscow, Peking, Rio de Janeiro, Bombay, and Baghdad." The screen cut away from the game to a shot of a vast mechanical clot of alien technology.

Jimmy Lee climbed out of the sofa and lumbered to the front door, not much more than pissing distance from where Fat Freddie and me remained seated. Jimmy Lee opened the door and looked out. "I don't see nothing." He shrugged, a confused look spreading across his bewhiskered face. He scratched himself. "It's kinda dark out, I guess. Maybe we'll see it in the morning."

"They didn't say one came to Dallas, you dumbass," Fat Freddie said. "Nearest one's probably that one in Los Angeles. You can't see there from here."

Jimmy Lee shrugged. "Could if it was big enough." But he sat back down, wriggling, I thought, to get away from the broken sofa springs.

Ferragamo completed another pass while Howard kept talking about the relative insignificance of football, using words like metaphysical, ethereal, mystical, and even Suey Generis, as if any of us was supposed to know who she was. He then said words that made all three of our jaws drop.

"We will be cancelling our usual halftime highlights to bring you Frank Reynolds in Washington, Max Robinson in Chicago, and Peter Jennings in London. They will update all of us on these transcendental developments that could affect every member of the human race."

"You gotta be shittin' me," Jimmy Lee said. "No highlights?"

Fat Freddie and I groaned. Howard hadn't been serious with that talk about football being insignificant. Anyone with half a brain could tell you that wasn't true. Football wasn't just significant; it was *life*. Howard had just been saying that nonsense for the schoolteachers and librarians who were listening. Hadn't he?

"Why don't they do this news shit during commercials?" Jimmy Lee asked.

"It's gotta be some kinda joke," I said. "Like April Fool's in December."

Then the TV screen showed the three broadcasters. Nope, not a joke. One look at Dandy Don's ashen face answered that question.

Jimmy Lee looked at me. "What's transcendental?"

Forget *transcendental*, I thought. I was still stuck way back on *preternatural*.

———

Even after the know-it-alls ruined halftime, they kept interrupting the game in the third quarter and then said good-bye to Howard, Dandy Don, and what's-his-name at the start of the fourth. I suppose that shouldn't have made me so mad cause the 'Boys was getting their asses whipped, but it did. Rule Number One in Texas is don't mess with the Cowboys.

Jimmy Lee got up and went home, slamming the front door on the doublewide on his way out. Fat Freddie decided to stay for a bit longer after some guy named Carl Sagan came on the TV to talk about the aliens.

"I saw him on PBS," Fat Freddie blurted out, then covered his mouth, his eyes wide. He looked sheepishly at me.

"PBS?" I asked. "You watch PBS?"

"There's this series called *Cosmos* that caught my eye."

"PBS? What has this world come to?"

Fat Freddie shrugged. "It's got good music," he said defensively.

"You watch PB-freaking-S for the music?"

"I dunno," Freddie said, shifting in his seat, looking like he'd just farted in church. "It's about planets and stars and stuff."

"PBS," I said. "Well, I'll be." I looked at Fat Freddie, realizing I had an honest-to-goodness alien in my own house. Didn't need no TV for that. "Never thought I'd see the day."

"Hey, Clete, do me a favor, will ya?" Fat Freddie said, leaning close and talking like it was some kind of conspiracy and don't let nobody else hear nothing even though we was the only ones in the room. "Let's keep this between just you and me. Don't say nothing to Jimmy Lee."

I just stared at him.

"Didn't you never watch Sesame Street?" Fat Freddie asked, his eyes shifting like a criminal.

"That's different and you know it," I said, and he knew I was right.

I stared at him, feeling like Perry Mason in front of a guilty witness.

———

The aliens didn't do a damned thing for the next week. They coulda done something while nothing but soaps was on or during the evening news, but no. They didn't do a goddamned thing. Just hovered over all the big cities—but not Dallas—like we was some kind of squirming bugs needing to be inspected underneath their microscopes.

For most of the week, that was about all you saw on the TV, all the smarty-pants experts telling us what to expect, most of them saying that these outer space critters must have come in peace else they'd have already blowed us up to kingdom come. That Sagan guy kept talking about *billions* of light years or something like that. All I know is it was *billions* and *billions*. I never could figure out what Fat Freddie saw in the guy.

Outgoing President Jimmy Carter didn't look like he knew whether to sneeze or take a shit. He kept saying that he would defer to "the president-elect" as if he didn't know the guy's name was Ronald Reagan. Myself, I thought Reagan would nuke the fuckers like I'd been sure he was gonna do to the Iranians if they didn't turn over the hostages before he got hisself sworn in. But Reagan looked as scared shitless as Carter, saying over and over, "Let's wait to hear their message. We trust that they came in peace."

I really didn't much give a shit until some candy asses started talking about cancelling the NFL games that weekend. Then other candy asses said the NFL should cancel the season —the *season!*—and the colleges should cancel all the bowl games.

"Can you believe that?" I asked over the phone to Jimmy Lee, who'd become the first guy to call now that Fat Freddie had put hisself on the Suspicious list. "What the hell would we do on New Year's Day without the bowl games?"

"Damned if I know," Jimmy Lee said. "Probably get drunk."

"And what the hell do they think they're gonna accomplish by cancelling the NFL?" I asked, hearing panic in my voice. "Hell, it's Cowboys-Eagles this week. If we win we're in the playoffs!"

"They can't cancel the games. The smarty-pants, girly men are just spittin' in the wind."

"If them aliens are gonna suck the life outta us, then let them fuckers try," I said. "Ain't no need for us to suck the life out all by ourselves. That's what cancelling the NFL season would do. That's what cancelling just this week would do. *Football is life!*"

"Preach it, Brother!" Jimmy Lee said.

We laughed just a little, but I was still steamed. "I don't much wanna watch TV at all now."

"I know what you mean," Jimmy Lee said. "If I have to see one of them news anchors one more time, I might have to kick in my TV set."

"That'd teach 'em," I said.

"Damned right," Jimmy Lee said.

———

I suppose we should be happy that the aliens didn't ruin the Cowboys game on Sunday, giving them a chance to beat the Eagles and get into the playoffs. Church was packed that morning and there was lots of hooting and hollering about sinnin' after Pastor Rick said that God was punishing us with them aliens giving us the evil eye because of our transgressions.

But I was sitting there mostly because Bobby Sue wouldn't go out with no atheists and if it meant I had a chance to get her in the back of my pickup, I'd go to church or let them aliens give me every evil eye they wanted to. But she didn't even want to look at me after service. She was too busy gabbing with her friends about the aliens. They was talking a mile a minute, mostly arguing over whether this meant the Rapture was about to happen.

Damn, I thought. Talk like that wasn't gonna make Bobby Sue cooperative.

So I went back home to worship in front of my TV set with Jimmy Lee and a fidgety Fat Freddie, who kept giving me nervous sidelong looks. Texas Stadium was full with Cowboys fans and they did lots of my kind of hooting and hollering, making noise about winnin,' not sinnin.'

With all due respect to Bobby Sue's panties which I may never get to hold in my trembling fingertips, I'll take my Sunday afternoons with Coach Tom Landry over Sunday mornings with Pastor Rick until the cows come home.

So like I said, the aliens gave us one last weekend of pure joy before they ruined the last Monday Night Football game of the year. The San Diego Chargers was playing the Pittsburgh Steelers and it would have been a mighty fine game to end the regular season if we'd gotten a chance to watch it. Fat Freddie arrived with the three steaming pizza boxes and for once, Jimmy Lee brought the Lone Star. It shoulda been great.

Howard and Dandy Don were in fine form during the pregame, clad in their gold ABC sports jackets that made them look like preachers of the Gospel of the two-minute drill. Even Frank Gifford looked okay as none of them had that frozen, nervous look they'd left us with a week ago.

"If I may opine," Cosell said.

"You always do, Howard," Dandy Don said, wearing his characteristic shit-eating grin.

"Many have pontificated about the reason for the alien spaceships over our great cities," Howard said. "They arrived during this very same broadcast a week ago and have yet to deign us with an explanation. Perhaps, as some have speculated, they are still rousing themselves from interstellar sleep. Perhaps, as others have feared, they are deciding on our fate. Or perhaps they already know that fate and are taunting us like the great Muhammad Ali during a title fight.

"Until they choose to make their appearance and unveil their intentions, I will ally myself with those who contend that these aliens have come to us with goodwill toward all men and women," Howard said. "They crossed the great interstellar space using technologies we can only hope to fathom in an attempt to commune with another sentient species.

"If, however, the aliens mean us unspeakable harm, they

will see that the peoples of Earth will come together as never before. We will answer any threat unified, responding as one because, in fact, we are one. One human race of many nationalities, languages, colors, and creeds. But in the end, we are one. And we will emerge victorious.

"I speak not for the diplomats of Earth, of course, but solely as one humble commentator."

Cosell blinked rapidly and fell silent.

"Humble?" Dandy Don gave Howard another shit-eating grin. "Howard, did you really say that?"

"Danderoo," Cosell said, "We all must be humbled at least a little by knowing that in the impossible vastness of space, we are no longer alone."

The telecast broke for a commercial. We all looked at each other, already washing down our second and third slices of pizza with our second and third Lone Stars. With every new cigarette, the blue cloud of smoke grew thicker.

"If they're gonna talk about this shit all night long," Jimmy Lee said, "I'm going home right now and blow out my brains."

"You ain't a good enough shot to hit that small a target," Fat Freddie said, almost choking on his slice of pepperoni as he yucked it up over his brilliant wit.

We enjoyed good fortune for less than a full quarter. Terry Bradshaw and Dan Fouts threw passes to Lynn Swann and Kellen Winslow. Franco Harris and Chuck Muncie ran the ball. And Howard, Dandy Don, and Frank actually talked about football. Imagine that, football. It felt like honey on a sore throat.

Then the goddamned aliens made their appearance, not descending from their spaceships or anything, and not even waiting until halftime. They just took over the TV set.

"Greetings to all humans," a voice said in a warm, familiar Texas accent. As if it was one of us. The screen filled with a view of Planet Earth from outer space, looking all blue except for the swirling whites of clouds. I realized that the alien voice was not coming from the TV set, which had fallen silent, but from within my own head.

"We have observed your species for a long time," it said. "Recently, we determined that corrective action was necessary because as a species you have stagnated. We are now interceding so that you may progress to the next level."

"What if we like the level we're at now?" Jimmy Lee asked, a sliver of pizza cheese hanging off his beard like a bright yellow booger.

Fat Freddie and I shushed Jimmy Lee silent.

"Individually, you waste exorbitant amounts of time on things that are not productive to you achieving your full potential," the alien voice said. "Many of you spend every waking hour attempting to mate."

"Mate? What are they talking about?" Jimmy Lee said. "I don't take but two or three minutes."

"While the need to reproduce is fundamental," the alien continued, "your mechanisms are hopelessly inefficient. We will guide you to processes that will free your energies to be spent in a more fruitful way."

I never much cared for people telling me what to do, but this alien was talking my language. If he and his people could show me a quicker way to get in Bobby Sue's pants, I was all for it.

"A second problem of your people," the alien said, "is your addictions that destroy your bodies and fracture your emotions. We will provide 'upgrades' that will eliminate these self-destructive impulses. You will no longer crave heroin or cocaine...."

Me, Jimmy Lee, and Fat Freddie nodded our approval and began lighting new cigarettes.

The alien continued. "Whiskey and beer will no longer hold

their grip on your souls. They will no longer kill your brain cells."

We looked at each other wide-eyed and quickly gulped down the rest of our beers.

"You will desire," the alien said, "only the amount of food that your body requires and you will prefer the healthiest alternatives."

Each of us dove at another slice of pizza.

"Tobacco products will become a thing of the past."

We simultaneously took in the deepest of drags.

"Finally," the alien said, its voice suddenly light and lively, "you will end your pointless pursuit of those things you call sports. Your energies and time will no longer be wasted on football, basketball, baseball, hockey, golf, and NASCAR. There will be no more World Cup soccer or the Olympics. All those silly games that you have thrown away so many hours on will be removed. It will be a shock at first, but eventually you will feel a burden lifted from your shoulders."

I realized my jaw had dropped wide open only when I saw Jimmy Lee and Fat Freddie in the same condition. Loose ash fell from the glowing tips of our unsmoked cigarettes.

I narrowed my eyes. "Who the hell do they think they are?" I roared. My fists clenched and I gritted my teeth.

"They're taking away everything that makes life worth living," Fat Freddie said.

"Yeah," Jimmy Lee said. "Fucking, food, and football."

———

The alien signed off, promising a new and improved human race, one ready to achieve its full potential. The TV returned to the football game, which appeared to have taken a long timeout during the alien's broadcast.

Howard began to talk, but I wasn't listening. The time for

action was now. I went to my tiny bedroom closet and on the shelf above where my Sunday suit hung, I retrieved my double-barreled shotgun. I grabbed ammo from the box on the shelf and loaded the shotgun.

"Clete," Fat Freddie said from the open bedroom doorway. My bed was unmade and the sheets smelled sour. "It ain't that bad. Don't do nothing stupid."

I walked past him and Jimmy Lee and kicked open the doublewide's front door. As I walked down the steps, I heard the two rustle along behind me. The air felt clean and cool. I walked until I stood beside my black pickup truck.

"What are you doing, Clete?" Fat Freddie asked.

I pointed my shotgun to the sky and imagined one of the alien spacecraft hovering above me. I aimed and fired, the kick almost blowing my shoulder off. The roar of the shotgun rang in my ears. I aimed again, this time more slowly, seeing in my mind's eye the spaceship's bulls-eye on its underbelly. I pulled the trigger.

I heard Fat Freddie and Jimmy Lee whisper.

"I'll get my gun," Jimmy Lee said. "I'll be right back."

"Me, too," Fat Freddie said.

Off in the distance, I heard a single report at first and then a second and a third and a fourth. They came from off to the South and then to the West and then in all directions.

It sounded like the Fourth of July.

And in a way, it was.

Them aliens might be pretty smart, I thought, but they were also pretty dumb. They didn't know us very well at all.

It was Day One of their rule and The Rebellion had already begun.

The history books will record that in Texas, you don't ever fuck with football.

POWER CHORDS

BRIGID COLLINS

Professional writer Brigid Collins is the daughter of professional writer Ron Collins. Clearly the incredible writing skills run in the family. She has sold many stories over the years, including some to Pulphouse Fiction Magazine *and to* Fiction River. *And as a team with her father, she sometimes is a guest editor for* Fiction River.

In this final original story in the volume, Brigid takes her love of music and gives us a fascinating and fun story of aliens and music. A perfect Pulphouse *story to end this wild anthology.*

Emma Carlton was reveling in the pure noise energy brewing between her and her guitar, marveling at the nimbleness of her own fingers on the fretboard, shivering at the gritty growl of the new distortion pedal she'd picked up at work yesterday, and most of all, thanking absolute fuck that her crotchety old neighbor Mrs. Sweeny was out of town so she could turn her amp all the way up without worrying about getting another noise complaint hurled at her.

She was sweating buckets, due to either the stifling corn-field-scented summer heat wafting in through the open garage bay door or the way she was throwing herself around and kicking at her equipment while she played, pretending she was Frank Iero at a high-octane concert—and with the new pedal, she almost had the sound right. She couldn't play as fast as him yet, but she was getting there.

Her blood sang in her veins, salt and garage grit coated her lips, her drenched-through tank top and short-shorts were slicked to her like a second skin, and the distorted chords poured out of her, via the guitar, and out into the orangey pink of early dusk.

She was *rocking*.

She was rocking, and for this one evening, no one could stop her. *Nothing* could stop her.

And then the space junk crashed through the garage roof and crushed her amp to smithereens.

"What the *fuck?!*"

Her heart, which had already been racing with the euphoria of playing, started pounding double-time. She leapt backward in reflex, landed on her foot wrong, and went crashing to the dirty concrete floor. Her guitar let out an unamplified and totally un-hardcore squawk.

Her tailbone throbbing, she struggled to sit up and disentangle herself from the guitar strap.

There was a whole bunch more dust in the air now, as well as bits of wood and shingle from the hole in the roof. A smell of singed stone filled the garage. A metallic ticking sound, like an engine cooling off, came from the middle of the floor, right where she'd had her amp situated.

Blinking grit and sweat from her eyes, Emma forced herself to take in the sight of the culprit: a twisted hunk of machinery the size of a mini-fridge embedded in the poured concrete floor. Little wisps of gray-white smoke curled up from it like the trails from incense sticks. The tangled power cords of her amp/pedal setup were splayed outward from under it like the legs of a huge, splatted spider.

"Aw, goddammit," Emma said. She set her guitar aside with arms that shook, then hauled herself over to inspect the damage.

"It's the fucking Russians, I just bet," she muttered. "Spy satellites peeking in on their little social experiment. Fucking guys think they own the country already. Think they can smash my goddamned amp and get away with it? I paid a lot of fucking *money* for that amp!"

By the end, her muttering had become shouting, and her inspection of the space junk with which the Russians had bull's-eyed her amp had turned into flipping double fingers up at the hole in her roof.

Chest heaving, arms shaking, Emma glared through that hole and just *wished* she could develop laser beam eyes right on the spot.

She didn't manage to shoot lasers from her eyes, but she did zero in on the trail of black smoke slowly spreading in the sky. She noticed, now that her guitar had been fucking *silenced*, a thin whistling sound, like a teakettle under the Doppler effect.

She followed the line of the smoke and turned to look out the garage door. Something was hurtling toward the cornfield across the way, giving off that teakettle shriek and spewing black smoke. As she watched, the object struck somewhere in the middle of the cornfield. A faint tremor under her feet followed.

"We'll just go take a little look-see, then," she said. She scooped her phone up from the wooden step leading up into the house and stomped down the driveway. "Get all sorts of photographic evidence, won't we?"

She supposed she should be weeping tears of sweet relief that the space junk had missed her car. She could afford another amp, and fixing the garage roof wouldn't be too difficult, but she couldn't have her car out of commission, or worse, totally destroyed. So she was lucky, really.

But she couldn't get the anger to flush out of her system. Every freaking way she turned, *something* was always trying to stop her from *rocking* it. Whether it was her parents with their stuffy ideas of turning her into a philharmonic player like them (what kid wants to admit she'd had ten years of fucking *harp* lessons?), her so-called friends who'd kicked her out of the band *she'd started*, goddammit (so *what* if she'd insisted they play nothing much other than every song MCR had ever writ-ten), or her only neighbor on this lonely stretch of farm road constantly calling the cops on her solo jam sessions (and why the fuck couldn't Mrs. Sweeny just take out her goddamned hearing aids, huh?), it all amounted to the same story. She wouldn't be surprised at this point if her landlord decided to blame the damage to the garage on her hardcore musical aspirations.

She was so sick of it. The goddamned Russians, or whoever was responsible here, were going to pay for this.

"Fucking wreck our country if you can, assholes, but you're buying me a fancy-ass new amp and a whole slew of pedals, and definitely that gorgeous new Fender I saw in Indy last month. That is fucking *happening*."

She crashed through the stalks of not-quite-ripe corn, spelling out more demands for restitution and snapping pictures of the smoke trail with her phone for documentation purposes, and didn't once think of the cliché of aliens in cornfields.

Not, that is, until she reached the crash site.

Even then, *aliens* weren't the first thing she thought of. The first thing she thought was that someone was playing a very cruel, very *weird* joke on her.

Standing in the middle of the cornfield was a harp. A full-size symphony harp, the exact kind she'd toiled away on for ten horrible years under her parents' strict gaze.

Of course, the harp wasn't the only thing in the field. Sitting on a bed of flattened and charred cornstalks was a thing that looked like a Greyhound bus, only with the fortification of a battleship and with no wheels that Emma could see. Its front end had driven itself into the ground, and though the dirt was churned up and plenty of corn had been uprooted, the vehicle itself showed little in the way of crumpling. Most of the damage seemed to have been done to the back end, which had been torn or blasted off. There were scorch marks running along the body, and the stink of burnt metal overrode the sweet corn scent. Emma covered her mouth and nose with the crook of her elbow.

"The *actual* fuck?" she said.

And that was when the harp moved, when it turned to point its sound box at her and crawled toward her on whip-like strings that whispered and zipped against the cornstalks.

<Play me, oh play me quick,> said a melodious, frantic voice in Emma's head.

Emma screamed, tried to run back the way she'd come, got her feet tangled in cornstalks, and went down with a jarring flump. Her phone bounced out of her hand and out of reach. Her teeth clacked together painfully.

For a couple dizzy breaths, she fully believed she'd imagined the whole thing. She had to've.

<Play me, quick! Before *they* come.>

That voice resonated in Emma's head just as if she had that sound box against her shoulder, right next to her ear. And if the voice itself didn't chase away her imagination theory, the harp strings winding around her ankles and shoulders sure as fuck did.

"Oh God oh God oh God," she chanted, struggling. This was it. Death in a cornfield, strung up by a space alien that had taken the form of her old musical nemesis. Fucking shit. When she'd screamed at her mom that she'd rather die than play the harp anymore, she hadn't meant *this*.

<Stop that wriggling and *play me*,> said the harp. <Or do you want to suffer the Silence from Space descending upon your ridiculous planet?>

The strings entwined around Emma's arms and legs lifted her from the dirt and turned her to face the harp. Emma stared at it with wide eyes. Strange, but she couldn't shake the feeling that there was a...a face, or at least eyes, staring back at her from the top of the sound box, right where the curved neck became the shoulder. It wasn't that there was anything carved or painted on the wood there, or that the grain had knots that formed an optical illusion. It was just a feeling she couldn't shake.

Emma realized that the harp had set her down, firmly but gently, on her feet. The strings were unwinding themselves from her, but slowly, as if the harp was ensuring she wasn't about to bolt the moment she had her freedom.

Not a freaking bad idea, Emma thought.

But when the strings had receded enough to let the blood rush back into her extremities, Emma held her place.

"You creamed my fucking amp," she said. The anger was running through her blood again, tingling in her fingers and her toes. "What'd you have to go and crash-land on my planet for, anyway?"

<Please,> the harp said. <I'm sorry. I can't drive the tourship by myself, but my friends are...all my friends are—>

The harp cut itself off. It didn't move, but Emma got the impression its gaze had shifted back toward the smoldering wreckage of the bus thing. Emma cut her eyes that way, too, watching the smoke grow blacker in the deepening evening. A sudden lump formed in her throat.

Oh, Christ. She was feeling sorry for a harp.

<The Silence from Space is following me. If they discover me, if the scouts that are chasing me find this planet, they will descend and devour everything that makes music. Your world will become one of the Damped. It may already be too late.>

Emma rubbed at her prickling arms. Suddenly, this Indiana cornfield was leached of its summer warmth. A world without music? "Oh, fuck no. *That's* not happening."

<Then play me. The computer on the tourship told me I'd find someone at these coordinates who was compatible. It must be you.>

"It's me," Emma agreed, though the words tasted sour. "I guess those ten years weren't for nothing after all."

The harp whipped a string out toward the wreckage and brought a piece of debris over for Emma to sit on. The metal was still hot, but not hot enough to burn the bare skin of the back of her thighs, just enough to be uncomfortably warm through her short-shorts. Once Emma was seated, the harp balanced itself awkwardly on her shoulder.

Her fingers found their places on the strings. A shudder of rebellious revulsion worked its way through her. The harp wobbled a little.

"Okay, what should I play?"

<Anything. Don't worry about being fancy, just be —oh, no.>

Emma felt the harp tense up. Unable to stop herself, she looked up.

Against the deep purple sky to the east, a long, yellowish shape was moving toward them.

<The Silence from Space,> moaned the harp. <We're too late.>

The yellowish shape came on fast. In the space of a downbeat, Emma could make out angular details, metallic doohickeys, and what was possibly an array of ray guns that marked it as a spaceship. In two fast measures, the ship was nosing its way straight for their little crash site in the cornfield.

<It's over,> said the harp as the Silence from Space landed their snot-colored spaceship beside them in a whirlwind that set Emma's ponytail flailing. The melodic tones in Emma's head grew ragged with sobs. <They'll Damp us like they did my friends.>

Emma thumped the harp's sound box with the heel of her hand. "Stop that. Jesus, and you called *my* planet ridiculous. Are you going to just roll over and let them do you like that? Are you going to let them get away with what they did to your friends?"

The harp hiccupped. <N-no...>

"When the crotchety neighbors of the universe call in a noise complaint on us, what do we do?"

The harp hiccupped again. <Play…louder?>

"That's fucking right, we do. We play until their ears bleed or our fingers do. Whichever comes second."

The spaceship's door opened with a hydraulic hiss straight out of every alien invasion movie Emma had ever seen. There was even billowing white smoke coming from inside. Any moment now, the BEAs would come shambling out, point their ray guns at her and command her to take them to her leader.

Setting her fingers firmly back on the harp's strings, Emma searched her brain for a harp piece to play, any harp piece, but all she came up with was *the* piece, the one she'd finally quit playing the harp over: a boring, stilted thing her mom in particular had insisted she master. She'd sworn she would never play that one again as long as she lived. *"Not even if I were dying and the only way to save my life was to play it,"* she'd told her mom.

And here she was, in a situation that sure looked a lot like life or death—two shadowy figures were materializing in the smoke-filled spaceship door, and Emma thought she could make out those ray guns held at waist-level. Damping guns, she supposed they were. If there was no more music in the world after this encounter, it might as well be death.

"RrrrrTime to be quiet," said one of the beings descending from the spaceship. Now that it had emerged from the smoke, its wrinkled, leathery green skin was visible, as well as its huge, clearly sensitive ears. The ears were bigger than an elephant's, and they flapped and flared like gills on a fish gasping for air in the bottom of a boat.

The big-eared scout raised its Damping gun and pointed it at Emma's head.

Luckily, Emma had just realized she could play whatever the fuck she wanted right now.

"Eat my riffs, dickweed," she said, and played the first song she'd taught herself to play on the guitar: "I'm Not Okay (I Promise)" by My Chemical Romance.

It sounded off. as. *fuck.* The harp was horribly out of tune, probably due to the crash landing. Not to mention it was a fucking *harp* when this song deserved to be played on an electric guitar distorted all the way to the sweet spot. She missed a lot of notes in the transition between instruments.

But fucking God, it was the most amazing run-through of it she'd ever played. She could feel the uncanny liveliness of the strings, the way they breathed, the way the harp undeniably had a mind of its own. She felt the harp rising to meet her halfway on the song, even though it clearly hadn't heard anything quite like emo music before. She'd never had a guitar this in sync with her. Together, they shredded.

"Arrrrrgh!"

The scout dropped the gun to clap both hands over its ears, but its hands weren't big enough for the job. The other scout stepped forward, his own gun held steady.

"RrrrI told you not to take yourrrrr prrrrrrrotective muffs off, rrrrridiot," it said. Its own ears were covered with a pair of the hugest, fluffiest, neon pinkest earmuffs Emma had ever seen. And that was including the time she'd seen Mrs. Sweeny out trying to shovel her own driveway last winter.

The second scout leveled its Damping gun at the harp.

Emma stopped playing. There were times when even the loudest rock 'n roll needed a few measures of silence. For effect.

"Rrrrrthat's morrrre like it," said the second scout. It stomped closer to Emma, keeping the Damping gun held out.

She let him come closer, closer, just a little bit closer, letting those measures of silence stretch and stretch until...

"Frank Iero kick!" she shouted, letting loose with her foot at the same time as she struck her furious downbeat. The gun went flying out of the scout's hands and disappeared somewhere in the stalks of corn.

The scout let out a rrrolling squawk of protest and staggered backward.

"Harp, can you do your string walk while we're rocking it?" she shouted over the music.

<I think so.>

"Then let's *jam,* baby."

Emma kicked the debris she'd been using for a stool away and started using the space of the crash site as her own rock stage, jumping around just the way Frank Iero would. The harp crawled on its strings with her as she moved with the music, flailing and head banging with every power chord she fired out into the night. Wherever the two scouts popped up in the darkness to try to shoot either Emma or the harp, they jammed their way over there and either kicked or stringed the Damping guns away again.

Finally, the harp managed to hook a string around the one scout's pair of earmuffs and rip them away, setting the scout howling under their musical barrage and running for the cover of its ship.

"Nice work," Emma said.

<This is for what you did to my friends!> the harp shouted after the fleeing scout.

But the hydraulic door was closing, and the ship was lifting off. They probably didn't hear the harp's final call.

<That's not good,> said the harp as the two of them watched the booger ship shoot off into the night sky. <They'll send for reinforcements, and the real invasion will begin. I'm so sorry I brought them to your home, but thank you for helping me fight them off this time.>

"No sweat," Emma said, arming a generous beading of the stuff from her forehead. "We'll find some way to send them packing when they show up next time. That was the sweetest jam session I've ever played. I'd started to think I wasn't made for playing with other people after my band cut me out, but I'd actually really missed it."

<I also enjoy playing with others. Would you continue to work with me as I repair my ship?>

"Sure thing. I—"

Something rustled in the corn nearby. Emma tensed, not sure what she should expect after her evening of battle of the space bands.

The first scout came stumbling back into the crash site, holding its ears bundled against its head and looking side-to-side.

"Rrrrroh, that jerrrrk! He rrrrleft me herrrre. He...he...rrrrhe *ditched* me!"

To Emma's surprise, the scout flopped onto the ground and began to cry some of the shrillest, most heartbroken sobs she'd ever heard this side of a toddler. She was almost tempted to cover her own ears. She didn't, though. Instead, she went over and crouched in the dirt beside the scout.

"Hey, uh. It's not so bad. That guy didn't deserve you, anyway," she said. "You could hang with us if you want."

The scout blinked up at her. "RrrrBut I trrrrried to Damp you."

Emma shrugged. "You won't try again, will you?"

"Rrrrnooo..."

"Cool. Wanna join our band?"

The scout blinked again, harder this time. "Rrrrjoin yourrrr *band?*"

<Join *our* band?> said the harp, sounding affronted. <She helped Damp my friends!>

"But she's got a real pair of lungs on her, and a great growly voice that'll do a fucking number on some metal lyrics. If we get her some super sound-cancelling headphones, I'll bet she can sing with us without hurting her ears."

The scout had stopped crying now. "Rrrrthat sounds...fun?

Rrrrl've neverrrr been in a band beforrrre. Rrrrno one everrrr asked me to join."

Emma clapped a hand on the scout's shoulder, then turned back to the harp. "Come on, Harp. We can't very well defend my home planet from the invasion of the Silence from Space without a vocalist in the group, right?"

<I...suppose not.>

"Then we'll all work together here. Gotta make some compromises if we wanna protect the planet. Peace, love, and punk rock, am I right, or am I fucking right?"

<You're fucking right, I suppose.>

The scout nodded, letting her ears unfurl. "You're fucking right."

Emma pumped her fist in the air. "That's god*damn* right."

Nobody, not her parents, not her cranky neighbor, not even music-hating aliens from *outer fucking space*, was going to stop her from rocking it. Nobody ever had, nobody ever would.

Now if only she could find a way to convince the harp to let her hook it up to a distortion pedal.

ABOUT THE EDITOR

Considered one of the most prolific writers working in modern fiction, *USA Today* bestselling writer Dean Wesley Smith published almost two hundred novels in forty years, and hundreds and hundreds of short stories across many genres.

At the moment he produces novels in several major series, including the time travel Thunder Mountain novels set in the Old West, the galaxy-spanning Seeders Universe series, the urban fantasy Ghost of a Chance series, a superhero series starring Poker Boy, and a mystery series featuring the retired detectives of the Cold Poker Gang.

His monthly magazine, *Smith's Monthly*, which consists of only his own fiction, premiered in October 2013 and offers readers more than 70,000 words per issue, including a new and original novel every month.

During his career, Dean also wrote a couple dozen *Star Trek* novels, the only two original *Men in Black* novels, Spider-Man and X-Men novels, plus novels set in gaming and television worlds. Writing with his wife Kristine Kathryn Rusch under the name Kathryn Wesley, he wrote the novel for the NBC miniseries The Tenth Kingdom and other books for *Hallmark Hall of Fame* movies.

He wrote novels under dozens of pen names in the worlds of comic books and movies, including novelizations of almost a dozen films, from *The Final Fantasy* to *Steel* to *Rundown*.

Dean also worked as a fiction editor off and on, starting at Pulphouse Publishing, then at *VB Tech Journal*, then Pocket

Books, and now at WMG Publishing, where he and Kristine Kathryn Rusch serve as series editors for the acclaimed *Fiction River* anthology series, which launched in 2013. In 2018, WMG Publishing Inc. launched the first issue of the reincarnated *Pulphouse Fiction Magazine*, with Dean reprising his role as editor.

For more information about Dean's books and ongoing projects, please visit his website at www.deanwesleysmith.com and sign up for his newsletter.

ACKNOWLEDGMENTS

Thank you to the following wonderful people who supported the 2017 *Pulphouse Fiction Magazine* Kickstarter Subscription Drive.

Steve Perry
Steve Jenkins
Valerie Brook
Woelf Dietrich
Christian Wood
Michael A. Burstein
Martin Greening
Lynette Aspey
Mary Jo Rabe
Nancy Sweetland
Denise Baker Gaskins
Jim Gotaas
Paula Meengs
Amy Browning
Anders M. Ytterdahl
Tasha Turner

Darragh Metzger
Tony
Dan 'Grimmund' Long
Wulf Moon
David Macpherson
Linda Banche
Lianne
M. L. Buchman
Ken Hattaway
Sharan Volin
Ryan M. Williams
Justin Burnett
Brian D Lambert
Thomas Bull
Andreas Flögel
Marianne Villanueva
Meyari McFarland
Amadan
Linda Bruno
Maralee Nelder
Jessica Doyle
Tony Hernandez
Pierre L'Allier
B.J. Baye
John Ordover
AJ Lemke
John Devenny
Debb & O'Neil De Noux
Doug Houseman
Vera Soroka
Chuck Gatlin
C Kobayashi
Cathy Green
Kate Pavelle

Leah

Willard A. Stone

Chuck Emerson

John Lorentz & Ruth Sachter

Paul McNamee

Eric Kent Edstrom

Stephanie Lucas

Keith Garrett

Keith Beals

Kristyn Willson

Dayle Dermatis

Risa Scranton

Piet Wenings

Mark Kuhn

Kathryn Goldman

David Macfarlane

Ron Vitale

Walter Hawn

David Bruns

Diana Deverell

Lois Malby Olmstead

Rob Menaul

Sean Mead

Mary Haldeman

AnnieB

Diane Sayer

Sam McDonald

Katherine Crispin

Skevos Mavros

Danny Evarts

Kai

Jaq Greenspon

Doug Red

Sara Litt

Simo Muinonen
Lisa Silverthorne
Kathryn Hodghead
Rick Lawler
Caryl Giles
Charles Pearson
C. Kirk
Darren Eggett
Lisa Owen
Blythe Ayne
Erik T Johnson
Kate MacLeod
Lillian Csernica
Ann Kellett
J Stuart Pratt
Sam Turner
D.V. Berkom
Greg Gorden
Jeff Metzner
Nancy Johnson
Robert Clemens
Joy Oestreicher
Christina
FredH
John Rogers
Donald Mark
Gary Piserchio
Richard Boulter
Anne J
Dawn Watson
Tanith Korravai
Cassidy Percoco
Marnilo C
Vito Michienzi

Jason Zippay
Terry gene, novelist
John M. Portley
Andrew Bain
Rob Voss
Lauren Gemmell
Lee French
Luigi Ballabio
Andy
Richard Parks
Gregory Lovell
Kev Partner
M. Mahar
Allan Kaster
Angela Penrose
Jamie DeBree
J.V. Ackermann
Geoff Palmer
A.J. Abrao
Rebecca M. Senese
J.R. Murdock
Christine Connell
Ashley Pollard
Steven Rief
John Winkelman
Steve R
Bill
Leigh Saunders
Christine
AM Scott
donald crossman
Louisa Swann
Brent Bissell
Rob Vagle

Sharon Rowse
J & M Lowry
Mark Leslie
I.G. Frederick
Rick Lohmeyer
Jeff Soesbe
Michael Kowal
James Husum
Eugenia Parrish
Teri Babcock
Debbie Nulf
Sean Roach
Ken Talley
A.R. Henle
Justin Johnson
Jennifer Brinn
John Haines
Robert McCarter
Mary Kennedy
Kate Rooney
Lana Ayers
Gerard Ackerman
Jane Reeves Newell
Werner Meyer
Stefon Mears
Travis Heermann
Ray Vukcevich
Simon Horvat
Gregory Wade Stitz
Christina York
Fred A. Aiken
Anonymous Reader
Patrick
Joshua Cooper

W.A. Brown
Damien Filer
Andrew Hatchell
James Beach
Harvey Stanbrough
Sabrina Chase
Melissa H. Taylor
Paula Whitehouse
Alexandra Brandt
Joshua Maher
Annie Reed
Ranveig Wallace
Sarah C
Felicia Fredlund
Trent Walters
J. E. Hopkins
coraa
Daphne Riordan
Gary Jonas
Chris Abela
Celine Malgen
Marcelle Dubé
Sheila Watson
Chrissy Wissler
Joanna Penn
Chong Go Sunim
Johanna Rothman
Rob Slater
Laura Ware
Danica Oakley
David Hendrickson
Angie Simon
Amy Laurens
kathryn mccloskey

Linda
Mary Fishler-Fisk
Camille Lofters
Linda Maye Adams
Katrina Tipton
Kenneth Norris
Carolyn Rowland
Mark Grant
Stuart Jaffe
John Payne
Sharon Reamer
Len Chang
Robert Battle
James Wisher
Anthony St. Clair
Lena Goldfinch
Christina Martin
Marie Laura
Kari Kilgore
Derek Miller
Keith West
Emily Williams
Michael and Nitu Gulati-Pauly
Stephen Couch
Matt Herron
David Brown
Catalyst Games
Johnny Pedersen
Tracy May Adair
Joseph Wrzos
Terry Mixon
Turner L.
Lynda Foley
Fran Friel

Lisa Satterlund
Steven H Silver
Todd Goetz
Sandra Hofsommer
Bonnie S Warford
Al Harris
R.F. Kacy
Joy Johnson
Karen Shannon
Bonnie Koenig
Michael Harbour
Lyndon Perry
Scott Tefoe
Michael Nisivoccia
Christel Adina Loar
Michael La Ronn
Ashley Pollard
Steve R
Christine
Louisa Swann
Sharon Rowse
I.G. Frederick
Michael Kowal
Teri Babcock
Ken Talley
Jennifer Brinn
Mary Kennedy
Gerard Ackerman
Stefon Mears
Simon Horvat
Fred A. Aiken
Joshua Cooper
Andrew Hatchell
Sabrina Chase

Alexandra Brandt
Ranveig Wallace
Trent Walters
Daphne Riordan
Celine Malgen
Chrissy Wissler
Johanna Rothman
Danica Oakley
Amy Laurens
Mary Fishler-Fisk
Katrina Tipton
Mark Grant
Sharon Reamer
James Wisher
Christina Martin
Derek Miller
Michael and Nitu Gulati-Pauly
David Brown
Tracy May Adair
Turner L.
Lisa Satterlund
Sandra Hofsommer